THE NEST

KENNETH OPPEL

ILLUSTRATED BY

JON KLASSEN

SIMON & SCHUSTER
BOOKS FOR YOUNG READERS
NEW YORK · LONDON · TORONTO
SYDNEY · NEW DELHI

SIMON & SCHUSTER BOOKS FOR YOUNG READERS

An imprint of Simon & Schuster Children's Publishing Division

1230 Avenue of the Americas, New York, New York 10020

Text copyright © 2015 by Firewing Productions, Inc.

Illustrations copyright © 2015 by Jon Klassen

For information about special discounts for bulk purchases, please contact Simon & Schuster Special Sales at 1-866-506-1949 or business@simonandschuster.com.

The Simon & Schuster Speakers Bureau can bring authors to your live event. For more information or to book an event, contact the Simon & Schuster Speakers Bureau at 1-866-248-3049 or visit our website at www.simonspeakers.com.

Book design by Lucy Ruth Cummins

The text for this book is set in Baskerville. The illustrations for this book are rendered in graphite.

Manufactured in the United States of America / 0516 FFG

10 9 8 7 6 5 4 3

Library of Congress Cataloging-in-Publication Data

Oppel, Kenneth, 1967–

The nest / by Kenneth Oppel ; illustrated by Jon Klassen.

pages cm

Summary: "When wasps come to Steve in a dream offering to fix his sick baby brother, he thinks all he has to do is say yes. But yes may not mean what Steve thinks it means"— Provided by publisher.

ISBN 978-1-4814-3232-0 (hardcover) — ISBN 978-1-4814-3234-4 (ebook)

[1. Wasps—Fiction. 2. Babies—Fiction. 3. Supernatural—Fiction. 4. Horror stories—Fiction.]

I. Klassen, Jon, illustrator. II. Title.

PZ7.O614Ne 2015 [Fic]—dc23 2014038101

For Julia, Nathaniel, and Sophia

*T*HE FIRST TIME I SAW THEM, I THOUGHT THEY were angels. What else could they be, with their pale gossamer wings and the music that came off them, and the light that haloed them? Right away there was this feeling they'd been watching and waiting, that they knew me. They appeared in my dreams the tenth night after the baby was born.

Everything was a bit out of focus. I was standing in some kind of beautiful cave, with shimmering walls like white fabric, lit from outside. The angels were all peering down at me, floating in the air. Only one came close, so luminous and white. I don't know how, but I knew it was a she. Light flowed from her. She was very blurry, not at all human-looking. There were huge dark eyes, and a kind of mane made of light, and when she spoke, I couldn't see a mouth moving, but I felt her words, like a breeze against my face, and I understood her completely.

"We've come because of the baby," she said. "We've come to help."

*T*HERE WAS SOMETHING WRONG WITH THE BABY, but no one knew what. Not us, not the doctors. After a week in the hospital, Mom and Dad were allowed to bring the baby home, but almost every day they had to go back for more tests. Whenever Mom and Dad returned, there were new bits of information, new theories.

It wasn't like a virus, something the baby would just recover from. It wasn't that kind of sickness. It might be a kind of sickness that never got better.

He might not talk. He might not walk. He might not be able to feed himself. He might not even live.

When the baby was first born, Dad came home to tell me about his condition. That there was something wrong with his heart and his eyes and his brain and that he'd probably need surgery. There were a lot of things wrong with the baby.

And there was probably stuff Mom and Dad weren't telling me—and they definitely weren't telling Nicole anything at all. She thought the baby was getting all its shots at once and that this was just normal—for a newborn to be visiting the hospital every day and often staying overnight.

At night I sometimes overheard my parents talking, words and little bits of sentences.

". . . very rare . . ."

". . . poor prognosis . . . they don't know . . ."

". . . degenerative?"

". . . no one knows for sure . . ."

". . . congenital . . ."

". . . we were too old, shouldn't have tried . . ."

". . . nothing to do with that . . ."

". . . the doctor couldn't say . . ."

". . . certainly won't develop normally . . ."

". . . doesn't know . . . no one knows . . ."

During the day Mom and Dad kept looking things up in books and on the computer, reading, reading. Sometimes this seemed to make them happy, other times sadder. I wanted to know what they were reading and learning, but they didn't talk about it much.

I had my angel dream in my head, but I kept it to myself. I knew the dream was stupid, but it made me feel better.

It was a bad summer for wasps. Everyone said so. We usually got them in August, but this year they were early. Dad hadn't even put up his fake paper nests. Not that they worked that well anyway. One year we'd tried these liquid traps, half-filled with lemonade to lure the wasps inside so they'd get stuck and drown. They'd pile up and up. I hated wasps, but even I didn't like looking at them in their soggy mass grave, the few survivors clambering over the dead bodies, trying in vain to climb free. It was like a vision of hell from that old painting I'd seen in the art gallery and never forgotten. Anyway, there were plenty of yellow jackets zooming around our table, mostly around the pitcher of iced tea. I kept an eye on them.

It was Sunday and we were all sitting out on the back deck. Everyone was tired. No one talked much. The baby was having a nap in its room, and the baby monitor was on the table, with the volume turned up so we could hear every breath and snuffle. We drank iced tea, with the umbrella shading us. Nicole was on the lawn, where Mom had spread out a big blanket for her. She was storming a LEGO castle with some action figures. She had her knights and her big box of LEGOs and her toy telephone. She loved that telephone. It was plastic and old-fashioned, and you actually had to dial the numbers with a kind of transparent wheel. It used to be Dad's when he was little, and it wasn't busted-up or anything. Dad said he'd been very careful with his toys.

Suddenly Nicole broke off from her attack on the castle and picked up the toy phone as if it had rung. She had a quick conversation, laughed once, then frowned like a doctor getting very serious news. She said "Okay" and hung up.

"How's Mr. Nobody?" I called out to her.

"Fine," Nicole said.

Mr. Nobody was a family joke. About a year ago, just before Mom got pregnant, we'd get at least one phone call a day that was just silence. Whenever we answered, there was no one there. Who was it? It was nobody. Dad complained to the phone company, and they said they'd look into it. But it kept happening, so eventually we changed our phone number, and that stopped it for a bit. After a few weeks, though, we started getting the calls again.

Nicole began calling him Mr. Nobody. Mr. Nobody got his jollies calling us and not saying anything. Mr. Nobody was just lonely. He was a practical joker. He wanted friends. Nicole started including him in her nightly prayers. "And bless Mr. Nobody," she'd say.

"Any good jokes today, Nicole?" I asked from the deck. "Any interesting news?"

Nicole rolled her eyes like I was an idiot.

Two yellow jackets circled the rim of my glass. I moved it, but they followed; they liked sugary drinks. I'd never even been stung, but wasps terrified me, always had. I knew it was wimpy and irrational, but when they flew near me, my head filled with hot static and I'd lash out with my hands.

Once, before the baby was born, we'd hiked up Mount Maxwell and were looking at the view, and a wasp came buzzing around my head and wouldn't go away, and I started running straight for the drop-off. Dad grabbed me and shouted that I could've been killed. "Get a grip!" he shouted. I always remembered those words when I saw a wasp. Get a grip. There were a lot of things I was supposed to get a grip on. I just wasn't much good at it.

A third wasp flew in, and this one had different markings. Instead of black and yellow, it was mostly white, with a few silvery gray stripes. It was the same shape as the others, just a little bit bigger. The two yellow jackets took off, and the white-and-silver one settled on the rim of my glass.

When I tried to shoo it away, it veered toward my face, and I pushed back in my chair so hard, it fell over with a bang.

"Steve, just leave it alone," my father said. "If you make a big fuss, they're more likely to sting you."

I couldn't help it. I especially didn't like it when they flew around my face.

"Where is it!" I said.

"It's gone away," said Mom.

It hadn't gone away. I could feel it crawling on my hair.

With a shout I tried to smack it off, and suddenly

I felt a precise searing heat in my palm. I pulled back my hand. In the fleshy part near my thumb was a bright red dot, and already the skin around it was feeling hot.

"Did you get stung?" my mother asked.

I couldn't answer. I just stared.

"Honestly," grumbled Dad, coming around to look. "Come on inside and let's give it a wash."

The bottom half of my hand started to feel fat, like it did when you came inside the house after a really cold winter day and started to warm up suddenly.

"It looks a bit swollen," Dad said.

Numbly I compared both hands. "It's way redder than the other one."

"It'll be fine."

I didn't feel fine. A big wave of heat flushed through me. It started in the center of my back and radiated across to my shoulders, then down my arms. I could feel my heart racing.

"I don't feel right." I sat down.

"Do you think he's allergic?" I heard my mom say in concern. She pointed. "Look."

I was wearing a T-shirt, and on my upper arm a blotchy rash had appeared.

"Is it itchy?" Dad asked.

"I don't know," I said numbly.

"Does it itch?" he asked impatiently.

"Yeah! It's itchy!"

Mom said, "His hand looks pretty swollen. You should take him in."

"You mean the hospital?" Just saying the word made me feel like electricity was jolting through me. My heart pumped. I felt hot all over. "Am I gonna die?"

Dad sighed. "Steve, you are not going to die.

You're panicking, is all. Okay? Deep breath, buddy."

I was glad Dad didn't seem too concerned, only weary; if he'd been as worried-looking as Mom, I might have flipped out altogether.

"We should just rent a room at the hospital," he said.

The hospital wasn't far, and the nurse who first saw me didn't seem to think I was very important. She gave me some Benadryl to drink, and we found seats in a crowded waiting room. Dad read a magazine, but I didn't want to touch anything in case there were germs. I looked around at the other people. Most of them didn't look too sick, but they were sick, or else why would they be here, and they might have something I could catch. Every fifteen minutes I went to the bathroom to wash my hands, and then slathered on hand sanitizer from the wall dispenser. I tried to breathe in little sips so I didn't take in too much hospital air. We waited a couple of hours, and by the time I saw the doctor, the rash on my arm was fading, and my hand wasn't quite as swollen.

"You had a mild to moderate allergic reaction," he said. Shadows sagged beneath his eyes. He didn't really look at me when he talked; I guess he'd looked at quite enough people that day. "But next time you get stung, it might be worse. So I'm prescribing an EpiPen for you."

I knew what those were. I'd been in the staff room at school once and seen an entire bulletin board pinned with Ziploc bags containing the names and photos of kids, and their EpiPens.

The doctor said to Dad, "You might also want to get him a course of desensitization shots. That way you won't have to worry about the EpiPen."

In the parking lot, when Dad got behind the wheel of the car, he gave a big sigh before turning the key in the ignition. It was the same hospital where the baby had been born. The same one Dad and Mom kept going back to almost every day.

We didn't talk much on the way home. I felt bad about getting stung and making him drive me to the hospital. He looked tired. He glanced over a couple of times and asked how I was feeling, and I said fine and he nodded and smiled. He patted me on the knee.

"Sorry I was short-tempered with you," he said.

"That's okay."

"We'll book you those shots as soon as we can."

I wasn't too crazy about getting a bunch of needles jabbed into me, but I said, "Thanks."

That night when I slept, I slept deep—and that was the first time I saw the angels.

I still get scared at night. When I sleep, I pull the covers right up over my head and leave only a little hole that I can breathe through—but not see through. I don't want to see what's out there. I've slept like this for as long as I can remember. It's embarrassing, and I never tell anyone about it. I have a lot of nightmares. One of the worst ones is that I wake up in my bed, still under my covers, but I know there's someone or something standing at the foot of my bed. I am too terrified to move, or call out, and then there's a sound like paper tearing and my blankets are yanked off my body. I can feel the weight of them disappear, the sudden sweep of cold air, and I know I am totally exposed to whatever is standing there. And that's when I wake up for real.

When I was little, I'd call out for Mom—it was always Mom—and she'd come and sit on the edge of my bed and settle me down. Sometimes she stayed and waited for me to get back to sleep; sometimes, though, after a few minutes she'd head back to her own room and tell me to call out if I needed her. And I'd wrap myself up and try really hard to get to sleep.

Back then there was a show on TV I liked, about secret agents who had a hidden lab. To get to it they flipped a switch and part of the floor slowly dropped down to their underground lair. I wished my bed were like that. So that whenever I was scared, I could just press a button and my entire bed would sink down, and then the floor would slide over top of me, and nothing could get past it. No one could break through. I would be completely safe and untouchable in my little nest.

But I didn't have a bed like that. So I'd listen to the house clicking and settling and doing all its night things, working the furnace, keeping the fridge cold, and all the other secret things it did at night. And I'd try to get back to sleep. But sometimes I couldn't. And I'd start feeling it again, that shape in my room, that thing watching from the end of my bed, and I'd call out again. And this time Mom would stagger in and do what I'd wanted her to do all along—ask if I wanted to sleep in their room for the night. When I was younger, I spent a lot of time in their bed. I slept beside Mom, right on the edge, trying to take up as little room as possible, because I didn't want them to stop letting me sleep there.

I'd never told any of my friends about this, ever. That I was scared of the dark. That I had nightmares. That I'd sometimes slept in my parents' bed.

The night after the wasp sting, I could feel the nightmare coming on in my sleep, like a thundercloud gathering on the horizon. A dark shape assembled itself at the foot of my bed, and just stood there, watching me.

But then the most amazing thing happened. There was a sound, a kind of low musical trill, and with it, points of light. I knew because I looked; for the first time ever I turned in my dream and looked. More and more tiny little bits of light surrounded the dark shape and landed on it, and the darkness started to dissolve and disappear, and I felt such relief.

Suddenly I was in a bright cave-like space, lying on my stomach, and in front of me was her voice.

"We've come because of the baby," she said. "We've come to help."

"Who's we?" I asked.

"We come when people are scared or in trouble. We come when there's grief."

I looked around at all the glittering creatures on the walls and in the air.

"Are you angels?"

"You can think of us that way."

I stood up. I tried to look more closely at the angel in front of me. Her head alone seemed as big as me. It was a bit like standing before that huge stuffed lion at the museum, except the mane and whiskers were all light, and the eyes were huge, and the mouth never moved. She was magnificent, and I wasn't sure she had a mouth at all, but I was aware, every time she spoke, of something grazing my face, and of the smell of freshly mown grass.

"Now," she said, "my first question is, how are you?"

"Okay, I guess."

She nodded patiently, waiting.

"Everyone's worried about the baby," I added.

"It's dreadful when these things happen," she

said. "It's common, you know. There's some comfort in that. You are not alone in this."

"No, I guess not."

"And your little sister, how is she?"

"She's a pain, as always." I was beginning to feel a bit more at ease.

"Ah, yes. Little sisters."

"I don't think she really understands about the baby being sick. Really sick."

"That's just as well. Your parents?"

"They're super worried."

"Naturally."

"And scared."

"Of course they are. Nothing's scarier than having a sick child, and one so newly born, and so vulnerable. It's the worst thing for a parent. That's why we've come to help."

"How can you help?"

"We make things better."

"You mean the baby?"

"Of course."

"No one knows what's wrong with him exactly."

"We do."

"Angels know everything?"

She laughed. "Everything is a tall order! But we know enough to know what's wrong with the baby. It's congenital."

"What does that mean?"

"He was born with it. Don't you worry—I know you're a worrier—it's not something you can catch, or get later in life."

I wondered how she knew I was a worrier. But I guessed angels knew all sorts of things without needing to be told.

She said, "It's just a tiny little mistake inside him, and we can fix that mistake."

"You can?" I said with a rush of hope.

"You know about DNA, don't you?"

I remembered it from science: all the little pieces inside each of our cells, like a spiral ladder, that made us who we were.

"Well," she continued, "sometimes the bits get mixed up. It's the tiniest mix-up, but it can lead to bigger problems. People are very complicated inside."

"When?" I asked. "When can you do all this?"

"Soon enough. You'll see."

And then I woke up.

I WAITED THREE DAYS BEFORE I TOLD MOM about the dream.

I wasn't going to at first, because I had a lot of weird dreams, and sometimes they seemed to worry her; so I'd stopped telling her. I didn't want her to worry. I didn't want her to think I was a freak. But today she was looking so tired as she fed the baby, I thought this one dream might make her feel better. She smiled when I told it, but it was a wistful smile. "You've always had the most interesting dreams," she said.

"Maybe it means things will be okay."

When I was little, she and Dad had sometimes gone to church, but they pretty much stopped a few years ago. The occasional Easter or Christmas. We didn't talk about God or anything. Nicole blessed people at night, and she must have gotten that from Mom or Dad. But Mom also read her horoscope every day; she said it was just for fun, so I didn't think she took it seriously. Once I'd heard her say there was more than us in the universe, but I wasn't sure what she meant by that exactly. Aliens, or some kind of supernatural forces, maybe? I didn't know if she believed in a god, though.

All I knew was that this dream made me feel better. Waking up from it, I'd just felt happier. It happened sometimes, a dream that cast a kind of hopeful light from the night into the daytime.

Mom was feeding the baby from a bottle. She'd

tried to breast-feed him, but he wasn't very good at nursing. Something about the mouth muscles not being strong enough.

Afterward the baby was sleepy, and Mom put him back into his crib. When I looked at the baby, here's what I saw: a baby. He looked normal to me, ugly, like a turtle, his neck all wrinkly. Tight little red fists. Nicole had looked like that when she'd been born. And I'd looked the same too, in the pictures.

Here's what the baby could do: He slept a lot. He made funny faces. He kicked his arms and legs. He stuck out his tongue. He cried. He made pterodactyl sounds. He was a noisy gulper. Sometimes he spluttered and choked, and Mom patted him on the back. He gripped your little finger with his fist. He looked at bright lights. He looked past you, and sometimes right at you. Sometimes his eyes were half-open; sometimes they were wide open and bright and curious. He kicked his skinny legs and struck out with his arms at nothing at all.

But when I looked at the baby, mostly what I thought of was all the things I couldn't see—all the things that were going wrong inside him.

I felt stupid having a babysitter. I didn't need one, but Nicole did, and I didn't want to have to look after her all the times Mom and Dad were at work, or taking the baby to his appointments.

Her name was Vanessa and she was a zoology student at the university. She was taking a course over the summer, and the rest of the time she worked for us. She spoke very calmly, and sometimes I wished she'd talk faster. I got impatient waiting for her to finish sentences. She lived in a basement apartment a few streets over. Her clothes had a musty, scalpy smell. Nicole really liked her. She said Vanessa was good at playing castle and talking about bugs and horses.

I was inside watching TV, where it was air-conditioned and there were no wasps. Dad had showed Vanessa my new EpiPen and where we kept it in the medicine cabinet of the downstairs bathroom.

Through the sliding patio doors, I could see into the backyard. Vanessa was on the deck. She walked to the table and poured a drink of lemonade for Nicole, who was on the swings. Then Vanessa stared at the wooden table and kept staring. Her look was so intense, it made my skin crawl.

I went to the door and slid it open. "What's the matter?"

"Shh." Without looking up, she waved me over. She nodded. There was a big wasp on the table. It

had pale markings, like the one that had stung me
a few days before.

"I've never seen one like this," she said.

"It's not a yellow jacket," I told her.

"Or a hornet. Hmm." She seemed genuinely
curious. "Maybe it's an albino. But it's definitely a
social wasp. A nester."

"How do you know?"

"Look what it's doing."

The wasp was scraping its head along the surface
of the table. There was a very faint clicking sound.

"You see its mandibles?" she whispered.

"Why's it eating the wood?"

"Not eating it. The adults just eat nectar."

"So what's it doing?"

"Collecting it."

Behind the wasp I saw a pale line where the surface had been scraped off.

"It takes a bit of wood fiber, mixes it with its own saliva, and then regurgitates it."

"Why?"

"To build the nest. Look, there it goes."

I took a step backward as the wasp lifted off and rose into the air. Almost in the next moment another insect landed heavily on the table. It took me a second to realize it was actually two bugs. The one on top was a big silvery wasp, and it was clutching a dead spider beneath it. The spider was bigger than the wasp, and it took the wasp a couple of tries to lift off again. Slowly, like an airplane with heavy cargo, it rose into the air with its kill, slewing off in the same direction as the first wasp. My breakfast lapped greasily against the sides of my stomach.

"Looks like you've got a nest nearby," Vanessa said, holding her hand to her eyes as she tracked the wasp.

It was high up now and didn't seem interested in stinging me, so I followed Vanessa as she walked along the side of our house, past Dad's favorite Japanese maple. We tilted our heads way back.

"See it?" she asked. "Waaaaay up there."

Under the eaves, right at the peak of the roof, was a tiny semispherical ball. A few shapes moved around on the outside. Our wasp disappeared inside.

"It's all different fibers from trees or plants or wood tables. That's why the nest can have several different shades."

"It's just kind of gray," I said.

I looked more closely at the wooden posts of our fence, and everywhere I saw little white lines. The wasps were eating our fence and table to make their nest.

"It's amazing," Vanessa said. "They're amazing little architects and engineers."

"I'm allergic," I reminded her.

"I know exactly where your EpiPen is."

The nest was above and to the right of the baby's room.

From down the street came the sound of a bell ringing. Nicole ran over, looking all excited.

"It's the knife guy!"

She bolted into the house so she could watch from the front door. Nicole was fascinated by him. He'd started coming around just this summer. He drove a strange stubby van without doors, slowly, ringing his bell, to see if anyone needed their knives sharpened.

Vanessa and I followed Nicole through the house. My little sister threw open the front door and stood on the porch, waiting. It was weird how excited she got about the knife guy. On the side of the van were lots of faded pictures of knives, and in big crooked hand-painted letters, the word "Grindi g"—because the last *n* was so worn out.

The van glided toward us. I didn't know how he made any money. I never saw a single person stop him and rush out with their kitchen knives. Last month, before the baby was born, Dad had flagged him down. I think it was just to give Nicole a thrill.

Nicole had stood with us at the curb as the van pulled over, and the knife guy stepped out in his coveralls. Before, I'd just glimpsed him in passing. He was an older guy, surprisingly tall, a bit stooped. His cheeks were hollowed out, and he had gray stubble for hair. He looked like his bones were meant for an even bigger body.

Dad had dragged his rotary lawn mower out from the garage—the blades were getting pretty dull, he'd said—and asked the knife guy if he could sharpen them. The guy gave a shrug, pursed his lips, and made a sound like, "Ehhhhhh," so we didn't know if he was saying yes or no. But then he went into the back of his van and came out with a screwdriver and removed the mower blades one by one.

Nicole watched everything, enthralled. The knife guy smiled at her as he took out the blades from the lawn mower, and then let her watch from the open back of the van as he sharpened them on his grindstone.

It wasn't until the end, when he was putting the blades back into the mower, that I noticed his hands. They were very large with big knuckles, but he had only four fingers on each hand, and they were weirdly shaped, and splayed so that they looked more like pincers.

Afterward Nicole said to Dad, "I guess he's not very good at his job."

"What do you mean?" Dad asked.

"He cut off his own fingers!"

Dad laughed. "He didn't cut them off, sweetie. He was born like that. I knew someone once who had the same condition."

"Oh," said Nicole.

"Anyway, didn't seem to slow him down any, did it?"

Dad ran the mower over a patch of the lawn, and grass clippings flew up, leaving a clean wake.

"Much better," Dad said.

Now, as Vanessa and I watched the van approach, Nicole looked up at us imploringly. "Can we bring him some knives?"

"I'm not sure your parents would want that, Nicole," Vanessa said. "We'd have to ask them first."

She sagged. "Okay."

As the van crawled alongside our house, the

knife guy leaned down over his steering wheel so he could peer out.

Nicole waved. The knife guy waved back, gave a big smile, and stopped. Maybe he didn't understand we had nothing for him today. I don't think his English was too good. He seemed familiar to me somehow, but not in a good way.

"We're okay!" I said. "Thank you!"

"Okay! Thanks you. Okay!" he said, and then he rang the bell again and kept moving on down the street.

When he turned the corner, I realized I'd been holding my breath.

That night at dinner Mom and Dad weren't talking much. When they'd come back from the hospital, they looked pretty serious, and I was afraid to ask them what had happened. Nicole didn't notice.

Between mouthfuls of mashed potato and fish sticks she talked about castles and metal and her favorite knight and all its special skills. Her phone was under her chair, like she was expecting an important call at any moment.

"Did Mr. Nobody have any good jokes today?" Dad asked her.

Nicole frowned, then shook her head. "He wasn't in the joking mood."

"Ah," said Dad.

"There's a wasps' nest on our house," I said. "Way up high, under the roof."

"Really?" Mom said.

"Vanessa and I saw it. Shouldn't we get an exterminator or something?"

Dad nodded. "Yeah. I'll call someone."

Mom asked, "Did you make the appointment with the allergist for Steve?"

"I'll do it tomorrow," Dad said.

"How's the baby?" I asked finally.

"We've got an appointment with a specialist. She's supposed to be very good. One of the few people who know about these things."

Nicole said, "And after that the baby'll be all better."

Dad smiled. "Don't know about that, Nic. But we'll know more anyway."

"I was sick when I was born too," she said.

"No you weren't," Dad replied.

Indignantly Nicole said, "Yes I was. I was yellow."

Dad sniffed out a laugh. "Oh, that was just jaundice. Postnatal jaundice. Lots of babies have it. It clears up in a couple of weeks."

Mom looked at Dad. "We were worried, though, remember? It seemed worrying. At the time."

I hated it when her eyes got wet. It made me scared. Like she wasn't my mom anymore but something fragile that might break.

After dinner, when Mom was giving Nicole her bath and I was helping Dad clean up the dishes, he said to me, "How are you doing, buddy?"

I shrugged. "Fine."

"A bit crazy around here."

"Is the baby going to die?" I asked.

He was doing a pretty lousy job arranging the plates in the dishwasher. Usually he was very particular.

"No, I don't think so. It's not like that, really. There's a lot that's . . ." He searched. "Not working like it should. And some of that they can treat. But a lot of it has to do with his level of ability and how he might develop in the future. Whether he'll be low-functioning or high-functioning."

"Low-functioning," I said. It sounded like something you'd say about a machine, not a person.

"I know, it's an awful term."

I rearranged a baking dish so it wasn't taking up half the rack. "So . . . we're high-functioning?"

He gave a small chuckle. "Supposedly. Though, some days it doesn't feel like that, does it?"

I was wondering if he was thinking of me. I definitely felt low-functioning sometimes.

"It's something to do with his DNA, isn't it?" I said.

He looked at me. "That's right."

"Congenital," I added. It made me feel better to have the words. As if knowing the names of things meant I had some power over them.

"Right. He was born with it. It's very rare, apparently. There aren't a lot of recorded cases yet. It only got named a couple years ago."

I was about to ask what the name was, but didn't. I wasn't sure why. This was a word I didn't want to know.

Later, when I was going to bed, Mom hugged me and thanked me for being so brave.

"I'm not brave," I said.

"I'm sorry we've been away so much. It won't be like this for always. . . ."

I didn't want her getting teary again, so I said, "We should do something about that wasp nest. I don't want to get stung again. And it's pretty close to the baby's room," I added, hoping that would make her take it more seriously.

"We'll take care of it."

"Did you ever believe in angels?" I asked.

She smiled. "When I was little, I think I might have."

"Not now?"

"I don't know that I do, Steve. It's a nice idea. But I don't think so."

Before I turned out my bedside light, I went through my two lists. First I read all the things there were to be grateful for. A lot of the time I felt pretty low, and I didn't know why really, and I thought this was a good way of reminding myself of all the good things in my life. The list was pretty long by now, about four pages torn from a notebook. Sometimes I added new things. The last thing was: Our baby.

Next was the list of people I wanted to keep safe. I didn't really know who I was asking. Maybe it was God, but I didn't really believe in God, so this wasn't praying exactly. It was a bit like how Nicole blessed people at night. This was me wanting to make sure that all the people I knew wouldn't get hurt. I started with Mom and Dad and Nicole

and the baby and then went through my grand-
parents and my uncles and aunts and cousins and
my friends Brendan and Sanjay. If I lost my place,
or started worrying I'd skipped someone, I began
at the beginning again, just to make sure. I always
ended with the baby, to make doubly sure I hadn't
forgotten him.

Then I turned off the light, pulled the covers
over my head, adjusted my breathing hole, and
slept.

I DIDN'T THINK I'D SEE THEM AGAIN, BUT that night I did. I was in the beautiful lighted cave, and my focus was a bit clearer this time. The walls reminded me of those rice paper blinds Brendan had in his bedroom. The cave's curved walls soared all around me. It felt good to be inside, like feeling the sun warm on your face through the car window even though it's winter outside.

And I was aware of the angels, moving about overhead, on the walls, on the high domed ceiling, wings aflutter, a pleasant thrum filling the air. And then, suddenly, one was much closer to me, and I knew instantly it was the same one I'd talked to before.

"Hello again," she said.

I still couldn't focus properly on her face. It was like that time the eye doctor dilated my pupils and I couldn't read anything or see anything close up. The angel seemed so near that she was just a blur of light. She was all black and white. I didn't feel at all afraid of her. Light radiated from her face. Her dark eyes were very large. No ears that I could make out. Her mouth was somehow sideways. Her face was divided by geometric patterns.

"How are you?" she asked me.

With each word I felt like I was being caressed, something very soft brushing my cheek, my throat.

"Fine."

"And your family. Holding up all right, I hope?" She was very polite.

"I think so." It seemed I should say something back. "How are you all doing?"

"Oh, very busy, as you can see. Very, very busy, as always."

"I didn't think I'd see you again."

"Well, of course you'll see us again."

I liked her an awful lot. She just seemed so easy and friendly—and I'd never been very good at having friends. At school I spent most of my time reading at recess and lunch. I did crosswords. I liked those. I didn't like the way kids talked to one another. I was not a very popular kid, never had been.

"We're here to help, and we'll stay until our work is done."

"Fixing the baby?" I said tentatively. I wanted to make sure I understood properly from last time.

"Absolutely. That's what all this is for."

There was a brief pause, and I looked around at the beautiful cave, and the light alone made me joyful.

"When will you fix the baby?"

"Very soon. Don't you worry."

"What I don't understand is . . ." I didn't want to be rude.

"Go on," she said gently.

"Well, how are you going to fix the baby?"

Would it be some angelic surgery? Did it involve spells or actual medicines or just words of power? Would they touch him with those magical gossamer caresses I was feeling now?

"Well," she said, "first of all, 'fix.' It's a rather odd choice of words, isn't it?"

I laughed with her. "Yes."

"We talk about fixing cars or a dishwasher. This

is a human being! The most glorious and complicated creature on the planet! You don't just go in there and repair him like an engine. It's incredibly difficult at the best of times."

"I'm sure it is."

"And in this case, quite impossible."

"Oh," I said, surprised. For the first time I realized I was standing on some kind of fibrous ledge, and if I peered straight down, I saw that the cave went much deeper and began to contract into a circle of bright light. There was a lot of fluttering activity down there, but the light was almost blinding. I preferred the softly filtered light through the walls higher up.

"I don't understand," I said. "You said you could fix the baby."

"'Fix.' 'Repair.' These are just words, really. Let's not get hung up on them. What matters is your baby will be perfectly healthy and well."

I nodded. "Okay."

"It's just not something you can patch up with a bit of string and sticky tape. No, no, no, we have to do this properly. Go right back to the beginning of things. Go deep. That's the proper way to do things. No half measures around here!"

"You mean going right inside the DNA?" I said, still not sure I was following her but wanting to sound knowledgeable, maybe even impress her.

"DNA—aren't you the clever one! Yes, good, you're on the right track. And we'll go deeper back still. That's where it will make the most amazing difference."

"So you can make him better," I said, relieved.

"Of course we can. Be careful, though." Her voice was softer, confiding. "There might be some people who try to get in our way."

I shook my head. "Who would do that?"

"You don't even usually see them, but you know they're there."

Immediately I thought of my nightmare somebody, darkly standing at the foot of my bed, and how just a few nights ago in my dream, the angels had come and burned him away like mist.

When I woke up, it was morning and I felt really happy. And then, waking up a bit more, I realized it was just a dream and no angels were going to fix the baby.

In the afternoon Vanessa brought a big plastic bag with some hunks of an old wasps' nest in it. She showed them to us on the kitchen table. Nicole got in there right away, touching everything. I held back. Looking at it made me feel like washing my hands.

"Is this supposed to make me less scared of wasps?" I asked.

She shrugged. "I just borrowed it from the lab. I thought you guys might be interested."

Inside were rows and rows of empty little hexagonal cells.

"It's like honeycomb!" Nicole said.

"Right," said Vanessa. "And it all starts with the queen wasp. She begins the nest. Sometimes it's underground, sometimes it's in a tree, or hanging from a branch, or under the eaves like yours."

"How does she make it?" Nicole wanted to know.

"It starts with just a little bit of wood fiber and saliva that the queen spits up, and she makes a little stalk from the roof, then a sort of umbrella, and on the underside, a few little paper rooms like these ones here. The queen lays one egg in each cell."

"And it hatches into a baby wasp," Nicole said.

"Well, yes, it hatches, but it's not a wasp right away."

She was just like a teacher, the slow calm way she talked. It irritated me, but what she was saying was actually interesting. "The egg hatches into something called a larva."

Nicole narrowed her eyes suspiciously. "What's that?"

"It's sort of white and wormy, and it doesn't look like much. It's just got a mouth and black dots for eyes, and all it does is eat and eat."

"What does it eat?" Nicole wanted to know.

"I'm glad you asked," she said, and she really did look glad. "Usually dead insects. The queen might go and chomp the head off a bumblebee and bring back the decapitated body. Wasps can kill insects much bigger than themselves."

"We saw one with that crazy big spider, remember?" I said to Vanessa.

"Whoa!" said Nicole, impressed.

"So the larva grows and grows and then seals itself inside the cell with silk. It doesn't eat anymore. And it's not called a larva anymore."

"It's a pupa," I said, remembering biology class. I wanted to show Nicole that Vanessa wasn't the only one who knew interesting things.

"Yep," she said. "And even though the pupa isn't eating anymore, it's changing inside. It's transforming. And then when it's all done, it cracks the seal of its cell! And it crawls out! A full-grown worker wasp!"

She did that last part really well, acting out a giant wasp muscling its way into the open, pretending her hands were a pair of hungry mandibles.

"Cool!" said Nicole, looking at all the cells in the nest. "There must be so many of those guys!"

"Except they're all girls," Vanessa said.

Nicole looked delighted. "Really?"

"Yep, every one. And then they start building the nest bigger, and feeding the new larvae."

"More dead bugs," Nicole said.

"Yes. Although, once they're adults, the wasps eat only nectar. And they pollinate plants when they do it. It's not just bees that do that. Wasps are important too. Our planet needs them."

"So what does the queen do now?" I asked. "Now that everyone's working for her."

"The queen just lays more eggs. That's it."

Nicole asked, "Do they all become queens?"

Vanessa shook her head. "These ones are all sterile."

"What's that mean?"

"They can't make baby wasps. But at the end of the summer, when the nest is all finished, the queen lays her last eggs. She makes some males and females who aren't sterile. And these females become new queens and start their own nests next year."

Finally I touched a hunk of the nest. It had a rustly dry feeling. "It's ugly."

Vanessa shrugged. "I don't know. I think it's sort of beautiful. Everything makes nests. Birds for their eggs. Squirrels make dreys to sleep in through the winter, bears make dens, rabbits burrows."

"We don't make nests," Nicole said, laughing.

"Sure we do. Our houses are just big nests, really. A place where you can sleep and be safe—and grow."

He came right to the door.

I was all alone in the house. Mom and Dad had taken the baby to the specialist. And Vanessa had left early, to drop Nicole off at a friend's house a couple of blocks away. I was supposed to pick her up in two hours.

I was reading in my room when I heard the handbell that seemed so out of place on a city street. I tried to get back to my book. It was one I loved, that I sometimes read when I wanted something fun to escape into, but I couldn't concentrate. I just heard the faint sound of the knife guy's van getting closer, and each peal of the bell growing louder.

My window faced the street, but I wouldn't get up to look. I just lay on my bed, the book a jumble of unreadable words. Another peal, and I knew the van was right outside my house. I waited for the motor sounds to fade, but when the bell next rang, it hadn't moved. The van's motor idled. I waited. Maybe someone across the street was getting him to do something. I felt like there was a shadow in my room, getting thicker.

When the knock came, my whole body jerked.

It was not a polite knock. We had an old-fashioned metal knocker, and it slammed against the plate three, four, five times.

I lay very still. I took a jerky breath into my stomach and tried to hold it, one, two, three, four, but I couldn't. I needed more air.

Slam! Slam!

Nightmare fear jolted through me. I wished the floor would slide open and my bed would go down and the panel would seal me in and keep me safe.

I gasped air and slid off my bed. I commando crawled to the window and pulled myself up to kneeling. I poked my head above the sill. I saw the houses opposite, a letter carrier going from door to door. When I lifted my head, I saw the street, and then the van at our curb. A little higher, and I saw our lawn and the path leading to the front door. There was no one inside the cab of the van.

The knife guy was definitely at my doorstep, hammering away.

Our next-door neighbor, Mikhael, was mowing his lawn, but he was wearing headphones and didn't even seem to notice the knife guy. A few cars passed by on the road.

Slam! Slam! Slam!

The noise made red electricity in my head. Paralyzed, I stared through the window, and finally I saw the knife guy walking back toward his van. Eyes just peeping above the windowsill, I followed him. Halfway down the path he suddenly turned and looked straight up at me. Right at me in my bedroom, like he'd known I was there all along.

With one of his misshapen hands he pointed at his van. With his other hand he lifted a knife and turned it to and fro so the light caught the blade. It wasn't like a normal kitchen knife. It was bigger and had a weird curve to it. He shrugged as if asking a question.

Desperately I looked over at my neighbor. He was still pushing his mower, facing our house now. He must have seen the knife guy by now! Why wasn't he calling the police? Maybe he'd decided it was just best to ignore a crazy old guy with a big knife.

The knife guy started to walk back toward my house, and I lost sight of him as he stepped onto our porch. I ducked down against the radiator, its metal cool against my cheek. My heart pounded so fast, I worried I might pass out. If he knocked again, I would run out the back and jump the fence into the next street.

But a few seconds later I heard the van motor deepen, and when the bell pealed again, it was farther away. Soon I couldn't hear it anymore.

I went downstairs, my knees watery. Warily

I looked through the tall skinny window beside our front door. Lying on the porch was the big, strangely curved knife.

"It's very odd," Dad said, looking at the knife. I'd brought it inside and put it in an old shoe box. Considering its size, it was surprisingly light. The handle had a good grip and felt . . . *right* in my hand. I didn't need to touch the blade to know how sharp it was.

"Why would he just leave it like that?" I asked.

"Maybe he left it as a sample," Dad said. "To show us how good his workmanship is. I don't know. He's from a different time. . . ."

"Do you think we should call the police?" Mom asked.

We were in the kitchen. Nicole was watching TV. The baby had fallen asleep on the ride home from the specialist and was in his car seat in the living room.

Dad grimaced and let out a breath. "He's just a strange old guy—"

"He wouldn't stop knocking!" I said.

"He was probably just hoping we had some more business for him. He can't be making much money. I was chatting with the Howlands—you know, at number twenty-seven—and I mentioned him, and they looked at me like I was crazy. Said they'd never even seen the guy. I feel like he's been on the street practically every week this summer."

"Well, he really freaked me out," I said.

Mom put her warm hand on the back of my neck. "That must have been scary."

"It was just the way he kept knocking and knocking."

"I'm going to put this somewhere safe," Dad said. "It's really sharp. Just leave it alone, all right, Steve? Next time I see him, I'll give it back and ask him not to knock on our door again." He looked at me with a sympathetic smile. "I'm sure he's harmless, but you were right not to open the door."

I didn't know how to explain it to my parents, but the knife guy felt familiar. He felt like a nightmare. Unexpectedly I thought of what my dream angel had said, about how some people might try to stop them from making the baby well.

And I thought, *What if he comes back for the knife?*

The bright walls. The thrum of music. The shimmer of wings, and the angel coming to greet me right away.

"Hello, hello," she said cheerfully. "I'm awfully glad to see you again."

She made it sound like I had a choice. "I just come straight here," I told her.

I liked how she touched my face when she talked to me, and I could see her a bit more clearly now. The big eyes really were enormous, without pupils or irises. They were just pure darkness. And there seemed to be, in the middle of her forehead, a smaller dark dot—maybe it was a third eye, I wasn't sure. On the top of her head were two particularly thick whiskers, bendy filaments of light, and it was one of these she touched to my face when she spoke. Like a kind of bridge that allowed us to communicate.

"Well, there's always a choice," she said. "Always a choice. How are things?"

"Okay."

"'Okay' is a terribly vague word. You can do better than that, a smart boy like you. How is your family, your sister? How is the baby?"

"Still sick, but they think an operation might help. They saw a specialist. He needs an operation on his heart."

"I see."

Some part of me was very aware I was dreaming,

so I was bolder than normal. "When are you going to make the baby better?"

"My dear boy, we're working on it right now. Around the clock. No lazybones here!"

"Really? How?"

"As we speak, we're tending to him and nourishing him and letting him grow. He's going to be so healthy. He's still very little, but oh, I can already tell he's going to be a real beauty!"

I smiled and thought of his little dinosaur sounds. "He's kind of cute sometimes already."

"Well, just wait until you see him properly. Wait till he's in the crib."

I didn't understand. "He's already in the crib."

"Not your new baby."

I frowned. "What do you mean, 'new baby'?"

For a moment it seemed all the musical thrumming in the cave stopped, the silvery wings stilled.

"We've already gone through this," she said. "That's how we're fixing him. We're replacing him altogether."

Replacing. Inside the lighted cave it was still silent, as if every angelic presence were waiting for my reply.

"But I didn't . . . that's not what I thought you . . ." I couldn't finish my sentence.

"Oh, Steven. Steven, don't worry. I'm sorry if I didn't explain it properly. It's completely my fault. Forgive me. It will all be seamless. One day—and it really won't be so very long; I know it seems to take forever when you're anxious about something— you'll wake up, and the proper baby will be there, that's all."

"But . . . where will ours go?"

"The new one will be yours."

I was shaking my head. "But the . . . the old one?"

Her head tilted. "I'm afraid I don't understand your question."

"This one, here, right now. He won't be here anymore?"

"What would be the point of that? You'll call him the same name, of course. He'll look identical. No one will know except us."

"But this new baby, where does he come from?"

"Well, we're growing him right now, aren't we? Right here in our nest, outside your house."

I WOKE WITH MY HEART RACING. THE INSIDE
of my mouth tasted bad. For a second I thought
I might throw up. Sweat beaded my face and
neck. I sucked air through my breathing hole, tried
to inhale like Dr. Brown had taught me last year,
my stomach a big balloon that I filled, counting to
four as I slowly exhaled.

I was still sickeningly hot, so I threw off my blankets,
and was relieved to see it was morning—just past dawn.
I knew I wouldn't get back to sleep—didn't even want

to—so I pulled on jeans and a T-shirt and went outside to the backyard. It was early enough to be cool still, though you could feel the heat already clenched up in the earth and air, just waiting to unfurl.

I walked along the side of the house and peered up at the nest. In the low light of dawn, it looked like a giant piece of dead gray fruit. It was definitely bigger than before.

It could easily hold a baby.

If the baby were all curled up tight, like in those sonogram pictures of a mother's womb.

And then my heart started to race again, because I was worried I was going crazy.

A baby growing in a wasps' nest.

That whole rest of the morning, I felt like I was sleepwalking. Vanessa made us sandwiches for lunch, and Nicole wanted to eat outside, so we took our plates to the table. I ate as quickly as possible, before the wasps could come and start bothering us, but Nicole's ketchup brought them fast enough. Nicole still wanted ketchup with everything. A grilled cheese sandwich, fish sticks, carrot sticks. And the wasps went crazy for that big red blob on her plate. The yellow jackets kept diving in, and then some of the pale ones showed up and chased the yellow jackets off. Two landed right on Nicole's plate. She didn't seem bothered.

But suddenly they made me furious. I shooed them off. They swirled around. One veered away, but the other landed back on the table. I grabbed my empty tumbler and lifted it high so I could smash the wasp into goo.

"Wait!" said Vanessa, and she took the tumbler from my hand, inverted it, and trapped the wasp underneath.

"What's that supposed to do?" I demanded angrily. "It'll just come back when you let it go."

Inside the tumbler the wasp angrily bashed itself against the sides.

"I'm not letting it go," she said. "I want to show it to my prof. Maybe she knows what kind it is."

Vanessa found an old margarine tub from our recycling bin, stabbed some holes into the lid with a steak knife, and skillfully transferred the wasp into it. She sealed the lid tight.

"There we go," she said.

I didn't want to dream about them again. I worried it meant I was going crazy. But that very night I ended up in the cave anyway.

Not as much light was coming through the walls now—they looked thicker, more fibrous. When I peered down from my ledge, I saw that the cave tapered inward, and the circle of light at the center was smaller than last time.

I didn't want to be here. I willed myself to wake up. I told myself it was a dream and I was bored of it and wanted out. But I went nowhere. I turned. Behind me in the tough papery wall was a tunnel, big enough to crawl through, but before I could even bend to peer into it properly, I felt a soft filament caress the back of my head. Despite myself, my body relaxed. A big breath seeped into my lungs. My shoulders dropped. I turned to face the queen.

"You were upset after our last conversation," she said. "You were upset all day."

"You're not an angel," I said. "You're just a wasp."

"Well, I prefer 'angel,' but 'wasp' is acceptable too. If that's what makes most sense to you. Names are just names. They don't really mean anything in the end."

I didn't really understand what she meant by that. It was like something from a textbook I wasn't smart enough to understand. I looked at her closely. Even in the dimmer light, I could see her face more clearly, and it was unmistakably a wasp's. What I'd thought was a silvery nose was a diamond of pigment. As for the sideways mouth, I'd been very wrong. It was the vertical gap between a set of mandibles. As I looked, they parted sideways a little, like pincers. They were sharp-edged.

Amazingly, I didn't feel scared of her. I was allergic and was in front of a wasp bigger than me. But I sensed instinctively she didn't mean me any harm. And anyway, wasn't this just a dream?

I looked to the top of her fine-whiskered head, at

the snaky antenna that bridged the gap between us.

"That's how we talk, isn't it?" I asked. "You touch one to me, and we understand each other."

"In part, yes. But also because I stung you."

My body had a quick nauseating memory. "That was you?"

"Indeed it was. I needed a bit of you in me, and a bit of me in you. It was you I wanted to talk to."

"Why?"

"Young people are much more open-minded. Your brains are still so beautifully honest and accepting and supple."

"I'm allergic, you know!"

"I do apologize."

"So . . . that's you up in the nest on our house."

"That's my nest."

"You're the queen!"

Just a hint of pride in her voice: "That would be me."

"And where I am now," I said, looking around, "this is the nest, isn't it?"

"Right again."

"It's a real place. But I thought . . ."

"What did you think?"

"That I just dreamt you."

"You are dreaming. But it's also real."

I wasn't sure this made any sense. "But how can I fit inside?"

"Your dream self can fit into any space," she said as if it were the simplest notion in the world. "Outside the nest you're big. Inside you're small."

Relief mingled with my astonishment. I wasn't crazy. These dreams weren't just imaginary. They were somehow welded to the real world, just like the nest was welded to our roof.

"We're as real as you are," the queen said. "Including the worker you killed today."

I blinked. "What? Oh, no. Our babysitter just caught one in a glass."

"And she took my worker somewhere and killed her so she could study her."

"How do you know that?"

"I don't consider it very kind. Do you?"

"Vanessa said her professor might want to study it."

"We have feelings! We have aspirations! We're not just little bugs."

"What exactly are you, then?"

She ignored me. "My workers live only four weeks. They're giving their lives for this baby. Your baby! You could be a little more grateful!"

"I didn't ask for this!"

"There's such a thing as manners. Imagine you're just going about your business and someone gasses you to death."

"Gasses! What do you mean?"

"That's what your babysitter did to my worker. Put her in a little chamber and poisoned her with gas."

It sounded terrible. "I'm sorry."

"I hope you are."

"I didn't know about any of this."

"It's like murder."

"Really, I'm sorry—but it wasn't me!"

"It's all right. She wasn't very important anyway." The queen chuckled. "Practically interchangeable, they are. Thousands upon thousands of them to do the work. Anyway," she added cheerily, "let's not let it happen again, shall we?"

She made me feel we were still friends, like I was automatically part of her team.

"It's bad for morale," she said. "How's your morale, by the way?"

"Okay," I said warily. I wasn't sure how much I should be talking to her anymore.

"Just okay?"

"I think so."

"Well, we'll change that, won't we? We'll get that taken care of."

"Look," I said, "I don't really understand what you're planning."

"Of course you do. You're a clever boy."

"This whole idea of the baby you're growing . . ."

"Exactly! It's our gift to you. Everyone likes a gift."

"Yes, but—"

"And everyone likes to be thanked for a gift."

I said nothing.

"Ah, well, you'll thank us later."

I blurted it out: "I don't understand any of this, but I don't want you doing anything to the baby!"

"You haven't even seen the baby yet," she replied. "We just finished the nest properly today."

I looked around. This place was nothing like

the bits Vanessa had showed us a few days before. "I thought nests were supposed to have rows and rows of cells."

"Well, this one is different. It has just one cell for just one egg. This entire nest is devoted to your new baby. That's all we'll grow in here. And look, the egg's just hatched. See up there?"

I looked and could see, at the very top of the dim cave, a pale blob.

I squinted. "I can't really . . ."

"I'll fly you up. Just hold on."

Before I could object, her antennae wrapped themselves around me and lifted me atop her head. Wings whirring, she darted off the ledge. Instinctively I shut my sleeping eyes tight, expecting that horrible amusement-park plunge, but I wasn't falling, just rising. My fear dissolved, and I opened my eyes and wanted to shout with exhilaration. After a few seconds we reached the top of the nest. Glued to the ceiling was a pasty slug-like creature.

"There's our little darling," said the queen proudly.

It was slimy, with two black dots sunk into the front end of its soggy body. Underneath the eyes it had a kind of hole, and it was eating. All around it, stuck to the nest ceiling, were insects—a dead spider, headless bees, and other things that I couldn't quite recognize, but there was a bit of something red that looked like it had hair on it.

"It's disgusting," I said.

"No, it's just a larva. It's just starting."

"I don't want to look at it."

For the first time the queen's voice was harsh; it came with a kind of clicking sound, like fingernails scratching at one another, which I realized was her mandibles opening and closing. "Shame on you! You shouldn't judge things by their appearances. I imagine you didn't look very appetizing when you were just conceived and starting to grow in your mother's womb."

I was still being held by her antennae, floating through the air, circling the larva.

"I want you to stop," I said.

"What on earth are you suggesting?" she said, clicking angrily. "That we harm the baby?"

"I want all of this to stop!" I repeated.

"Oh, that's quite impossible. Now that it's started."

"I'm waking up now."

"Only if I say so," said the queen, and her antennae released me, and she tipped me off her head.

With a surge of terror I fell, away from the larva baby, down through the nest. I woke with a jerk in my bed. My blanket was on the floor, as if someone had yanked it off me.

"The wasp you caught yesterday," I said to Vanessa when she arrived in the morning.

Her eyes lit up with excitement. "I was going to tell you guys about that."

"Did you kill it?"

"Oh." She looked a bit surprised at the question. Her clothes smelled mustier than usual. "Well, yes, in a killing jar. That's how we get all our specimens, Steven. We just put them in a jar with a little ethyl acetate—it's like nail polish remover, and it konks them out."

"Kills them."

She nodded, looking at me uncertainly. "Does that upset you? I thought you—"

"Hated wasps. Yeah, I do." It wasn't the fact that she'd killed it. It was the fact that I already knew, because my dream wasp, the queen, had told me.

"Are you okay?" she asked.

"Uh-huh. So . . . what kind of wasp was it?"

Her face got all eager again. "I still don't know. My prof wasn't there, but I showed it around to some of the other people in the lab, and no one could identify it. I said maybe it's just some kind of albino, but no one had ever really heard of an albino wasp, so . . ."

I felt the familiar prickle of electricity start along my upper back, threatening to radiate out my arms. "Really?"

She nodded. "And the more I looked at it—I think there's something strange about its structure."

"Its body?"

"Yeah." She frowned. "The proportions of the head, thorax, and abdomen, and some of the connective structures, they're not like other wasps'. . . ."

For a moment I stopped hearing her, because

my heart was beating in my ears, and I felt the day's heat hard on my face.

". . . it might not even be a wasp," Vanessa was saying.

"What is it, then?" I asked, and I guess I must've sounded a bit panicky, because she looked at me strangely again.

"Well, we'll see what my prof says."

"The doctor said it was a wasp!" I said. "He said I got a wasp sting."

"Well, lots of things sting. I mean, I'm just an undergrad, Steven. I don't know much about insects at all. It might be a new species, or just a variation that's not been noted before around here. We'll see."

*T*HE BIG LADDER WAS IN THE GARAGE. DAD used it to clean out the gutters in the fall. It was pretty light, and I didn't have much trouble carrying it around the side of the house. I unfolded it and notched the safety hinges. I'd climbed up only once before, and that was with Dad standing at the bottom, holding on.

I bumped it along the wall so it was right underneath the nest. It didn't reach all the way. There was still a big gap. That was why I had the broom.

I figured that from the top of the ladder I'd be able to reach up and knock the nest off. It would fall and smash on the ground. All the wasps would swarm out. But I'd get down the ladder as soon as possible and pelt inside. I had my EpiPen in my pocket, just in case.

I was home alone. Vanessa had taken Nicole and the baby down the street for ice cream and then to the park. I'd said I was staying at home to read. I'd been home a lot this summer. We hadn't planned a vacation, because of the baby, and my day camp didn't start till August. Brendan and Sanjay were both away someplace or other.

I started up the ladder. After a few rungs I felt the legs shift a little, but it still seemed pretty stable. It was funny. I was afraid of a lot of things, but heights wasn't one of them. Even though I had scary dreams where I was stranded on top of skinny poles, or razor-thin ledges, I liked climbing trees and going up glass elevators, and standing on the see-through floor of the CN Tower.

I wore a long-sleeved shirt, with a hoodie over it, the hood pulled tight, leaving only a small circle for my eyes and nose. As I went higher, the ladder clicked and creaked. With my left hand I held tight to the side; with my right I gripped the broom. I was aware of the wasps flying past overhead, to and from the nest.

With every rung I got angrier. My parents couldn't even deal with the nest. I was allergic, but they were too busy. They were busy with the baby and would be for the rest of their lives, so I had to do it. I didn't know if these wasps were really from my dreams, but I wanted them off my house. I wanted them out of my dreams. That nest was coming down.

I didn't go all the way to the top. I stayed two

rungs down, so I had something to hold on to. With the broom I reached as high as I could, and still it didn't come anywhere near the nest.

I mounted another rung. Now I had to reach down to hold on to the very top of the ladder. The broom came closer, the bristles just shy of the nest's underside. I knew I didn't have long. More wasps were gyrating around the nest now.

I was just off to the right of the baby's window, and there was a stone sill that stuck out a little bit, so I took hold of it in my left hand. I stepped onto the top rung. The ladder swayed and then settled down. My chest leaned against the brick wall, and I felt my jerky heartbeats, but it made me feel safer, something so solid against me. Tilting my face up, I slowly raised the broom, straining for the nest. I didn't know how strong a swing I could give it without losing my grip—or my balance.

First swing, and the bristles gently raked the bottom of the nest. The broom kept going. Grunting, I brought it back and tried again. It hit a little harder this time, and I saw some papery bits waft down.

The wasps came. In a rush they dropped from the bottom of the nest and swarmed around the bristles of the broom. I gripped the very tip of the handle and was preparing to give it a big upward shove, when I was suddenly aware of a single wasp on my left hand, then a second on the knuckles of my right. I froze.

Another landed on the little exposed circle of my face. I felt its tiny legs, the flex of its solid body. I didn't yell. I couldn't. All my instincts—to swat and flail about—had somehow been paralyzed. I was terrified they would sting, but they didn't. They just stayed put. They were all over the broom now, crawling toward me.

I let the broom drop. It clattered down the side of the ladder to the ground. The wasps swirled, and more landed on me, my clothing, my hands, my face, just staying very still. I wanted to reach for the EpiPen in my pocket, but I was afraid the wasps on my hand would sting if I moved. The ones on my face were blurry blots in my vision. But I knew they were there, motionless, their antennae pricked attentively, watching me with their compound eyes, smelling me.

I took a downward step. Some of the wasps left my hands. I took another step. A few launched themselves from my forehead. Step by step more of them left. By the time my feet touched the ground, there wasn't a single one on me.

I looked up and saw the last of them disappearing back into the nest.

A neighbor had seen me up on the ladder and called my parents.

"Who was it?" I asked when Mom and Dad confronted me after dinner. I'd tried to be really careful and make sure no one was around in their backyards.

"Their English wasn't good," Dad said, shrugging. "I don't know."

"But that's not important," said Mom with forced patience. We were down in the kitchen. Nicole was already in bed. "What made you do something so dangerous?"

I felt myself dig in. "I was careful. I wanted the nest down. What's the big deal?"

"For starters, you're allergic!" Mom said.

"I had my EpiPen," I muttered.

"You get stung enough times, that's not going to help," Dad said.

"Well, maybe if I got some desensitization shots!" I told him.

"We're a little busy around here, buddy," Dad said, and I could tell by the look in his eyes, he was getting angry. Mom put a hand on his arm.

"Yeah, well, I'm allergic!" I said. "And no one seems to care about that!"

"We do care—" Mom began.

"So just stay inside until we take care of it," Dad said. "You don't climb a ladder!"

"What if one gets into the house?" I demanded. "What if I get stung that way? What if the baby gets stung?"

They didn't say anything for a few seconds, but Dad's eyes were still fierce.

"You could've fallen," Mom said. "You could've really, really hurt yourself. . . ."

"We'll take care of the nest," Dad said.

Mom came toward me and tried to hug me, but I shrugged her off.

"What's going on, Steven?" she asked softly. "Tell us what's up."

I turned away from her because I could feel my throat aching, and I didn't want to cry. I looked at the wall, at the print with its brushed silver metal frame. I felt all the words welling up inside me, and I didn't want them inside me anymore.

I told Mom and Dad about my dreams. All the conversations with the angels who'd turned out to be wasps. I sat on the kitchen chair and stared at the floor, partly so I could concentrate and not forget anything, partly because I was afraid to see my parents' faces. I told them how the queen had said she was going to replace our baby with a new one growing in the nest, a healthy baby, and how I didn't think the dream was real, not really, but

I was sick of hearing from her, and I just wanted them all gone.

Neither of them interrupted me, and when I finally looked up, I wished I hadn't. Dad's chest was moving in and out slowly and deeply. Mom was crying, tears running down her cheeks, and then her face crumpled and she was sobbing. Dad went and put his arms around her and whispered something into her ear.

"It's too much," she said. "I can't . . ."

I sat rigidly, wishing I hadn't told them at all, wishing I could take it back.

Mom wiped her eyes and reached for me, and this time I let her hug me, just so I didn't have to see her face. "I know this has been a really hard time. I'm so sorry if we haven't been around much for you."

"It's okay. It's not your fault or anything."

"Do you want to talk to Dr. Brown again?" Dad asked.

I chewed at my lip. Quietly I said, "What if it's true?"

"You've always had pretty intense dreams," Dad said.

"I know, but—Vanessa said those wasps weren't normal."

"Well, that may be," said Dad, and he sounded like he was getting angry again, "but that doesn't mean a thing, Steven. I'm going to have a word with her, if she's encouraged any of this—"

"She hasn't!" I said. "Don't be mad at her."

I didn't want to talk anymore, because I saw the fear in their eyes, and that made me afraid. Someone told me once that if you worried you were crazy, it meant you couldn't be crazy. Because crazy people apparently had no idea they were crazy; they thought it was normal, walking around naked and yodeling. As I'd told my dreams aloud, I knew how insane they sounded—but I also remembered everything from those dreams, and they seemed so real.

Dad took a breath and tried to sound casual. "Maybe you should talk about this with Dr. Brown."

"You think I'm crazy again," I said, and this time I was crying.

Mom squeezed me hard. "You were never crazy. You were anxious, like a lot of people, like a lot of kids, and you're also imaginative and sensitive. And wonderful." She kissed the top of my head. "So wonderful."

I felt tired suddenly, in her arms. "I'll go talk to Dr. Brown," I sighed. "But I want you guys to get rid of the nest."

*D*R. BROWN HAD ALWAYS LOOKED A
little unstable to me. It was his eyebrows. They
were gray and bushy and got pointy at the
ends and angled sharply upward. I wondered if he
knew. You'd think that if your job involved talking to
crazy people, you'd make a special effort not to look
crazy yourself. Sometimes his breath smelled bad, like
old coffee and maybe cigarettes. I guess if you talked
all day, your mouth got kind of dry and nasty. His
voice was soothing, though, and he had a friendly
smile.

"So, it's been a while since we talked," he said. "I think almost a year. And we were talking about some challenges you were having, and some strategies for coping with them."

"Yeah."

There was a very thin file folder on his desk, closed. He must have checked it earlier. I remembered that he never took notes while we talked. I suppose he did that later, alone in his office, going "Hoo-wee!" and "Cray-zee!" and shaking his head.

"Did you find any of those strategies useful?" he asked me.

I told him that I'd tried to make my bedtime lists a bit shorter, and I wasn't washing my hands quite as much. Which wasn't entirely true. But it was summer, so it was harder for anyone to tell. In the winter, when it was awfully dry and cold, my hands got all chapped and red, especially around the knuckles. They looked really sore, and sometimes the skin would crack and people would comment on it, like I had some kind of skin disease. Right now they looked okay. I told him I'd been practicing deep breathing.

"Great! And how was your year at school?"

On the drive in to school, I used to silently name the same landmarks so I wouldn't have a bad day. I had a relaxation tape I liked to listen to in the car. At school I drank only from a certain water fountain, and I washed my hands between every class. I also had hand sanitizer with me, just in case. Pretty much every day I worried I might feel sick and throw up in the middle of the hallway in front of everyone, and then no one would be my friend anymore.

I told Dr. Brown the year had gone okay and I'd gotten better at cutting down some of my rituals, and worrying less about throwing up.

"Okay. Good. Your father told me some of the things that have been happening at home. It sounds pretty challenging. How do you feel about things?"

So we talked a bit about the baby and all the visits to the hospital and the doctors and how the house was sad.

"And how about outside home. What're you doing this summer?"

"Not much. Just hanging around."

"You're seeing your friends?"

"They're mostly away." I'd seen Brendan a few times, but we didn't really have much in common. He was always so happy and energetic that he made me feel lousy about myself. I was okay being alone. Anyway, I didn't know how to talk about the baby with anyone. *Except the queen*, I thought suddenly.

"And you've been having bad dreams, your dad said."

"Does he think I'm crazy?"

"No. They're worried about how hard this whole thing has been on you. You used to have a lot of nightmares, I recall."

I nodded.

"And there was also some sleepwalking, I think."

"Just a few times."

"There was one nightmare in particular. Do you remember it?"

Of course I remembered it. "There's something standing at the foot of the bed, just watching me. And sometimes they pull the covers off me."

"Okay. So tell me about these latest nightmares."

I let out a big breath and told him what I'd told Mom and Dad. How they hadn't felt like normal dreams at all.

"They certainly are very interesting," he said. "The wasp, does she have a name?"

"Is that important?"

"No, it's just that you keep saying 'she' or 'the queen,' so I was wondering if she had a name."

"I never asked. She never told me."

"How many conversations have you had?"

"Four."

"I remember us talking, last time, about how you had an imaginary friend when you were younger."

"Henry."

"Henry, that's it. And you talked to Henry until . . . grade five, wasn't it?"

"Not very much by then, only sometimes." I remembered what Dr. Brown had told me a year before, and I repeated it now. "It was really just a way of talking to myself. You know, helping me think things through."

"But when you stopped talking to him, you felt very lonely, you said."

It wasn't normal to have an imaginary friend in grade five—that's what Sanjay had told me, and he'd told James, and then it seemed pretty much everyone in my class knew. And so I'd had to stop talking to Henry.

I felt an unexpected tug inside my chest. "Yes."

"And now? Do you still miss him?"

"Not really," I lied. It wasn't exactly a lie. It wasn't so much Henry I missed; it was having someone like him, only real, to talk to. The perfect listener, the person who could help me sort things out.

"I remember," the doctor said, "when we last spoke, you had a very interesting expression for how you felt sometimes. I wrote it down because I thought it was so expressive. 'All in pieces.' Do you remember that?"

I hadn't—not until he'd said it. But now it came back, the feeling it described. Like I had a hundred shattered thoughts in my head, a hundred glittering bits of stained-glass window, and my eyes just kept dancing from one piece to the next without understanding what they meant or where they were supposed to go.

"Have you been feeling that way again?" Dr. Brown asked.

"A bit, I guess. Not exactly the same."

"Does the wasp, the queen, ever talk to you when you're awake?"

"No! Only when I'm asleep."

"Your father said you tried to knock down the nest. He was worried you might have fallen, or gotten stung."

"Yeah."

"That dream you had, where the queen said they were replacing the baby . . ."

He didn't finish the sentence, which I knew

meant he wanted me to talk. What I said would be important. But I didn't say anything. I was afraid that whatever I said would be wrong.

"It was a dream," I said finally.

"It was enough to get you up on that ladder."

"I'm really afraid of wasps," I said.

"But you decided to get very close to the nest."

"I just wanted . . . I wanted things to stop. I was angry at Mom and Dad for not doing anything or getting me my shots." This seemed normal. This seemed reasonable.

Dr. Brown looked at me pleasantly, waiting to see if I had anything more to add.

"The dreams just seemed . . ." I trailed off.

He smiled. "Well, there are many different theories about dreams. The important thing to remember is it's just a dream. They can feel like very powerful experiences, but they aren't true experiences, and they have no real power over you. It's sort of like that thing we talked about last time, do you remember? A feeling is not a fact. What happens in a dream stays inside the dream."

"Okay," I said. And then I told him something I'd kept back from my parents. "Except the queen told me something that came true."

"What's that?"

"That Vanessa had killed one of the wasps. I didn't know that. But the next day she told me about it."

Dr. Brown rocked his head from side to side. "Well, you know Vanessa is a biology student. You know she wanted to study the bug. That's what happens to bugs so we can study them."

"She said the wasp was unusual. That maybe it wasn't a wasp at all."

He smiled. "I was in the museum with my kids

last weekend, and there was a sign. I think it said there were five to fifty million species on the planet, and only one million have been discovered. Something like that. Amazing stuff."

"I guess so," I said, and thought about whether I should say the next bit. "When I was trying to knock down the nest, a whole bunch of wasps swarmed over me, but they didn't sting. None of them."

"Lucky."

"It was like they were just warning me. And as soon as I started going down the ladder, they flew off."

"I'm not a wasp expert. I know they're very territorial. Maybe when you were far enough away from the nest, they stopped seeing you as a threat."

"Maybe," I said, and let out a big breath. I actually felt better. "I don't want to dream about them anymore."

"Well, I'm pretty sure you can't control that.

Likely you'll have some more dreams about them, the nest, and the baby. There's a lot going on in your life right now, but with time the dreams will fade. Are you able to wake yourself up from them?"

I shook my head. "I tried once and it kept going."

He nodded sympathetically. "By the way, what's his name?"

"Who?"

He chuckled. "The baby. Your new brother. You've never said his name."

"Oh. Right. Theodore. Theo, we call him."

"Good name. Would you like to talk again in a couple of weeks?"

"Sure," I said.

Three days went by without me dreaming about them, and I felt hopeful. Maybe they were gone for good.

On Monday, Dad went into work and Mom went to the hospital by herself to talk to the specialist about the upcoming surgery. Vanessa was over for the afternoon, watching Nicole and the baby. We were in the living room, and she'd just given the baby his bottle.

"Do you want to hold him?" Vanessa asked after she'd burped him.

"Okay," I said nervously. I hadn't held the baby much. I was ashamed to admit it, but I was worried I'd get contaminated somehow, that what was wrong with him would become wrong with me. It didn't make any sense; I knew that. But I still felt it. Reluctantly I put my arms out, and Vanessa gave him to me.

Nicole was the one who was always all over the baby. She loved the baby. To her the baby just meant this wonderful happy new thing in her life.

She said once, not long after the baby had come home, "Just let me bask in his glory!"

It always made me feel mean when I watched Nicole with the baby. Because when I looked at him, I saw all the things that were supposed to be wrong with him; and I saw Mom looking tired and worried; and I saw Dad staring out the window, sometimes just into the distance, sometimes at our driveway, where the car was.

Nicole ran off to play, and Vanessa said: "Your mother was telling me about the operation."

"Yeah."

"Poor little bambino," said Vanessa. "He'll be just fine."

"He's all busted-up inside," I said.

"Busted-up," said Vanessa, considering.

"Yeah. It's not just his heart. There's a ton wrong with him. He could die."

"But no one knows for sure."

"Not now, but one day . . ."

Vanessa said, "One day things could go wrong with any of us."

"I guess."

"Lots of people have broken bits," she said. "I've got some inside me."

I looked up at her. "What?"

"It's called polycystic kidneys. My mom has it too. I found out when I was in high school. You start getting all these fluid-filled cysts on your kidneys."

"Is it bad?" I asked.

"It's slow, but it gets a little worse every year. Sooner or later my kidneys will probably stop working."

"Then what happens?"

"I'll need a kidney transplant."

I didn't know what to say. Vanessa grinned and

playfully pushed my shoulder. "Don't look so terrified, Steven. It's not for a long time. Anyway, my sister
says she'll donate one of hers, which is pretty great."

"And you'll be fine then." I felt like Nicole when
I said it, a little kid wanting a quick and reassuring
answer.

"For a while. Transplanted kidneys don't last
forever. But who knows what'll happen. Anyway,
'busted-up.' What's that mean? Lots of people I
know have something or other wrong with them.
A friend of my uncle's just got told he has MS. He's
only twenty-seven. No one knows what's going to
happen down the road. All I'm saying is, sooner or
later we're all busted-up in some way."

The baby was warm against my chest. I knew I
was broken too. I wasn't like other people. I was
scared and weird and anxious and sad lots of the
time, and I didn't know why. My parents thought I

was abnormal, I was pretty sure. They said I wasn't, but you don't get sent to a therapist if you're normal.

Sometimes we really aren't supposed to be the way we are. It's not good for us. And people don't like it. You've got to change. You've got to try harder and do deep breathing and maybe one day take pills and learn tricks so you can pretend to be more like other people. Normal people. But maybe Vanessa was right, and all those other people were broken too in their own ways. Maybe we all spent too much time pretending we weren't.

I held the baby, and he was small but not as light as the last time I'd held him. Because he was sickly, I always imagined I'd barely feel his weight, that he would float up and away. But in my arms he was surprisingly solid. I thought about what was inside, all the wet weird things we have in our bodies that make us work. And then deeper still, all the little squirmy cells and inside them the threads of DNA that tell everything what to do. And with the baby I pictured them like strings of Christmas tree lights, only some bulbs were missing, and others were winking, and some had blinked out for good.

And I didn't know what was going to happen or what it all meant, or what I was supposed to do about it.

"No one's perfect," Vanessa said, "that's all I'm saying. Your brother seems to have a lot wrong with him right now. But it might not always seem that way."

I knew I shouldn't ask, but I couldn't help it.

"That wasp you took," I said, "did you learn anything else about it?"

Vanessa looked uncomfortable. "Hey, you know, I'm sorry if I got you all freaked out about the wasps. Your dad wasn't too happy about it.

He said you tried to knock down the nest."

"That wasn't your fault." I hoped Dad hadn't said anything mean to her.

"It was a stupid thing to do," she said.

"I know!"

"Anyway, he asked me not to talk about it anymore."

"Oh." For a minute I said nothing, but then I felt angry. "I won't tell him anything. I'm just curious what it was."

"You promise you won't tell him?"

"Promise."

"You're not going to do anything else stupid with the nest?"

"No! So, what are they?"

"I showed it to my prof, and she agreed she hadn't seen one like it. She pinned it and took some pictures, but when she started to dissect it, there, uh, wasn't much of anything inside."

I swallowed. "What do you mean?"

"It just kind of collapsed, like an empty shell."

Whenever I got a panic attack, it almost always started the same way. There was a hot flush in the nape of my neck, and it would travel down my back and then out my arms, and sometimes my legs, like I'd been struck by lightning. And then came the feeling that I was going crazy, that I'd end up curled into a little ball and never, ever be right again.

"Probably I just put too much ethyl acetate in the killing jar," Vanessa was saying. "I might've dissolved it."

"Yeah," I said, trying to take a big breath into my abdomen.

The wasps weren't normal. They weren't filled with the normal stuff.

After dinner that night the baby wasn't interested in his bottle, and his little body seemed really floppy.

"Maybe it's the heat," Dad said. It was blistering outside, and even with the air-conditioning on, it wasn't much better inside.

"He's not right," Mom said, and she seemed really worried. Dad drove them to Emergency.

Nicole and I watched television, and I kept letting Nicole have more and more cookies until Dad came back.

"They're keeping him overnight," he said. "Mom's staying."

"Is he okay?" I asked.

"They think it might just be a virus."

"Like a cold," Nicole said, still watching television.

Dad ruffled her hair. "Right."

After Nicole was in bed, I asked Dad, "Is it serious?"

"They're not worried about the virus too much.

It's just . . . he needs to be strong for the heart surgery, and he needs it soon. But they don't want to
risk anything until he's as healthy as he can be. We
just have to hope for the best."

"Okay," I said.

He hugged me good night, told me to get some
sleep, told me he loved me. As I was coming back
from the bathroom, I glimpsed him sitting on the
edge of his bed in his underwear, taking his socks
off. His head was lowered, and I could see the patch
where he was losing his hair. He got one sock off
and massaged his toes and then seemed to forget
about the other sock. And then he wasn't even mas-
saging his toes anymore. He was just sitting there,
not looking at anything at all.

In bed I did my lists. I said my sort-of prayers twice,
because I was worried I might have missed someone.
Without Mom and the baby, the house felt lonelier.

I pulled the covers over my head and wrapped myself up like a cocoon.

Inside the nest it was dimmer than ever, but my focus was the clearest yet. Suspended from the ceiling was a big gauzy bundle of white that looked like silk and spit and cobweb. It took up nearly half the nest and gave off a fierce heat. When I peered down from my little ledge—had it been built just for me?—I could see, just outside the circular exit, a swarm of worker wasps hovering and beating their wings, angling cool air inside the nest. I felt the breeze against my face.

"The baby's pupating."

It was the queen, her antenna grazing me. I hadn't even heard her coming. Her wings were noiseless.

"He's not a larva anymore," she said. "The baby's eaten all he needs for now. He's spun a little nest around himself, and he's just concentrating on growing."

I tried to peer inside, but the baby was sealed away within its white cocoon. I thought of myself asleep in bed, all wrapped up in my blankets.

"I didn't know if you'd come back," the queen said to me.

"I don't seem to have a choice."

"Oh, of course you do, my dear. Of course you do. You want to come. That's why you're here."

I wasn't at all sure about this. But I felt differently now. If Dr. Brown was right, this was just a dream. It felt real, but it wasn't. It had no power over me.

"So, what happens next?" I asked.

"Well, the baby will grow, and then he'll be ready."

"To replace our baby."

"Goodness me, you're doing it again. This, right here, is your baby."

"Our baby needs a heart operation."

"He's in the hospital right now," said the queen. "I know. He'll be home in the morning. Your mother will be very sad indeed. She'll try to be brave, though. They'll have told her they can't perform their surgery until the baby's stronger. And very crude surgery it is, if you don't mind me saying. They do their best, don't get me wrong, best intentions and all that, but it's still primitive. Be loving to your mother. Because the fact is, the baby won't ever be strong enough to have the operation."

"You don't know that!" I said, and had to remind myself none of this was real.

"He doesn't have long. The doctors will be vague. They'll say, 'Oh, when he's stronger.' Maybe they'll even believe it themselves."

"You're sure?"

"It's very sad. But he doesn't have long. How are the others bearing up?"

I felt like my head was being crammed full of crumpled bits of paper, and I was trying to unfold them all to read the answers, but the printing was too small and the paper too torn. Nothing made sense.

I muttered, "Nicole doesn't really understand."

"Merciful. And your father?"

I thought of him sitting on the edge of the bed. "I don't think I've ever seen him sadder."

"And you?"

"What about me?"

"Who's taking care of you?"

"I'm fine."

"Who's looking after you? Who has a tender word for you?"

"They do; they're just tired."

"Of course. They must be shell-shocked. Shattered. Every parent's worst nightmare."

Defiantly I said, "But you're here to make everything better, right? To make a healthy baby."

"Of course. But we couldn't do it without you."

"What do you mean?"

"When I stung you, it was so I could talk to you, yes. But there was another reason. We took a little bit of you, a little bit of your DNA. Just to help us get the baby started. It's not just any old baby, remember. It's your family's."

"So . . . the baby's going to be a twin?"

"Oh, goodness gracious, no. We take care of all those little things once we have the raw ingredients. But we still need your help in another way."

"How?"

"We're clever, but we can't do everything. There's a point where we'll need you."

"Why don't you talk to my parents about it?"

"Out of the question. They're far too busy. Adult minds get so cluttered."

"None of this is up to me!" I was forgetting myself again. This wasn't real, any of it.

"No?" she said. "You're more important than you think."

I couldn't help being curious. "What would I do, anyway?"

"Right now you don't have to do a single thing."

"So when?"

"We'll let you know. Right now all you have to do is say yes."

This was new. So far in my dreams all I'd been doing was listening and watching. Like dream TV. Now I was being asked to do something.

"Have you noticed you never call the baby 'Theodore'?" the queen said.

"How did you know his name?"

"I know everything you know. You've never once called the baby 'Theo.' Why do you think that is?"

I shrugged.

"You're not ready to give him a name because you don't know if he'll live. It's a bit like admitting he's not a real person. And he's not, is he? Not yet. Not until we're done. I think you know what that means."

"What does it mean?"

"That you're ready to say yes."

"But what am I saying yes to?"

"'Yes' is a very powerful word. It's like opening a door. It's like fanning a flame. It's the most powerful word in the world."

The queen was maddening, the way she talked, the way words poured out of her and spiraled around.

"But you're still not telling me—"

"'Yes' means yes and everything that entails. We'll finish the baby, and you'll go into his room one morning and there he'll be, and he'll be healthy and it'll be like the old one was never there."

"As if my parents wouldn't notice!"

"No one will ask questions," the queen said. "You think they'll care when they discover he's healthy? You actually think they'll wonder, 'Hmmm. How can he be so healthy all of a sudden? How worrying! How suspicious!' They'll just be so grateful. And it will be Theo. Just healthy. And before you know it, you'll forget all about that crappy little broken baby."

I felt like I'd been slapped. Those were the first unkind words she'd spoken.

"That's mean," I said.

"Sometimes the truth hurts. Now, just think how

happy your parents will be. They'll be so happy, and everything will go back to the way it was. Happy, happy, happy."

"Happy . . ." I suddenly caught the smell of freshly cut grass again, felt a cooling summer breeze.

"That's right. And all you have to do is say yes. Yes to the end of suffering and heartbreak. Yes to making your mother and father happy. Yes to making a better life for everyone."

I thought, *It's just a dream anyway.*

I thought, *It has no power over me.*

I thought, *Why not?*

"Fine," I whispered.

"I'm sorry. I didn't hear that."

"Yes," I muttered.

"More clearly please."

"Yes, then! Yes! Yes!"

I was aware of a vast welling sorrow in my chest,

like a huge breath I didn't know needed exhaling. I was crying.

"There now," said the queen kindly, and her antennae brushed my tears away. "There, there. Let the sadness out. You've done the right thing, Steven. Such a brave, wonderful boy. Thank you."

And I cried, and woke, my blankets all tangled up around my breathing hole, smothering me. I pulled my head clear and sucked in air. For a moment I was confused and couldn't remember what had happened. When I did, I felt sick in my stomach. I'd done something terrible. I'd said yes. I'd agreed to help the wasps replace the baby.

Breathing deep, I tried to calm myself. Dr. Brown had said dreams felt very powerful but they weren't real experiences. Right now this didn't make me feel one bit better.

I whispered to myself, "I didn't mean it."

Like I was hoping someone would reply. Like someone would forgive me.

"I didn't mean it," I said again.

"I didn't mean it," I said fiercely, teeth pushed against my pillow.

*A*T AROUND ELEVEN THE NEXT MORNING, Dad went to pick Mom and the baby up from the hospital. The baby was crying and seemed more energetic. Mom looked wiped out, but she smiled and said it was amazing anyone could get better in a hospital with all the beeping and buzzing and people coming in and out at all hours.

"How is he?" I asked.

And Mom told me everything the queen had told me in my dream—almost everything. "When he's stronger, he'll have the operation. Maybe as soon as this week. But the doctors said he can stay at home till then. We just need to take extra care with him and make sure he doesn't get all limp again, or his fingernails or lips get blue. And then, with a bit of luck, he'll have the operation."

"And then he'll be all better?" asked Nicole, running her truck back and forth over an action figure.

"He'll be better," Mom said. "Not all better. There's always going to be things . . . different about him."

It was the first time Mom and Dad had really said that to Nicole. I watched her, wondering what she'd do. She shrugged.

"He looks fine to me," she said, and went off to find a different action figure to maul.

"Is it risky, the operation?" I asked Mom.

"It's complicated, but they're so good at these kinds of things now."

She smiled bravely, and I gave her a hug and said I was sure everything was going to be okay, and I tried to sound as reassuring as possible. Just like the queen had told me.

Dad made lunch, and we ate it inside. They were doing it for me, because of the wasps. The baby had taken a full bottle and was having a nap upstairs. Mom had the baby monitor set up nearby.

"I called an exterminator," Dad told me. "They're coming Friday to take care of that nest."

It was Tuesday. That was in three days. I nodded. "Thanks."

"Soonest I could get," he said. "They're crazy busy this year. It's a terrible summer for wasps."

We were cleaning the dishes when we heard the crying. We all stopped, and the back of my neck went electric. It was normal baby crying, but it was not a sound we'd ever heard from our baby. He was quiet. He'd never really cried. At most he made a gentle kind of bird trill. Blaring over the monitor right now was a big full baby wail.

Eyes wide, Nicole said, "Is that Theo?"

Mom and Dad were both rushing for the stairs. I followed. I took the stairs two at a time to keep up. When I entered the baby's room, Mom and Dad were leaning over the crib, peering down. The baby was deep asleep, breathing evenly, little hands balled into fists.

From downstairs we could still hear, faintly, the sound of a crying baby over the monitor.

"Weird," I said.

Dad picked up the transmitter part of the monitor and switched the channel. From downstairs the noise stopped.

"We must be picking up someone else's monitor," he said.

"The new people next door have a baby, don't they?" Mom said.

Dad nodded.

I knew it was crazy, but I couldn't help thinking it wasn't the baby next door. It was the baby outside our window, growing in the nest.

That night Mom and Dad closed their door all the way, but I still heard them talking. I think they talked about me a bit, because I caught Dr. Brown's name, and then I'm pretty sure they were discussing the baby. When I crept down the hall to hear better, Mom was telling a dream she'd had the night before in the hospital. In the dream a nurse came and told her that there'd been a mix-up and they'd given her the wrong baby, and the nurse had the right baby, and there was nothing wrong with him, he was healthy. And I couldn't really hear what else

Mom was saying next, because she was crying, but I heard her say the word "ashamed," and Dad's low soft words were covering up her choky little gasps.

It was very dark in the nest now. I could barely see the walls, and then I realized it was because the baby had grown so large, it was blocking out most of the light. I felt its presence all around me, though I could make out only its outlines. The nest was very humid. Last winter we'd gone to the zoo and visited the rain forest pavilion, and it had been really crowded with people in their puffy coats, and all the monkeys and gorillas and their thick animal smell and their food and their poo. It was overpowering, and I'd had to go outside to breathe in the icy air. It was like that now in the nest.

Almost at once the queen was before me. I didn't

want her touching me with her antennae, but I knew it was the only way we could talk.

"Delightful to see you, as always," the queen said. "So nice of you to drop by."

"Was that the baby we heard today?"

She gave a little hop of excitement. "Quite a set of lungs he has on him, yes?"

"It scared us all."

"A healthy wail, that's all, not like the sickly little bleats from that one in the crib. Oh, but I am so glad you heard him! He's crying out to you, to let you know he's ready to be born and loved by you all! He wants to meet you more than anything. He's growing just as fast as he can! Would you like to see him?"

"I don't—"

"Oh, come and see the baby! You can't see him at all from down here. It's too dark. There's better light higher up. I'm sure you'll fall in love with him."

Once again I felt myself taken hold of and lifted. As we moved closer, I was aware of the baby's impressive mass. I realized that, from below, all I'd seen were the shadows of a back and bottom and legs. Now, suddenly, at the very top of the nest there was light and I was peering down at the baby from above.

Gone was the silky covering. From the ceiling the baby hung suspended on a narrow stalk that looked like an umbilical cord, except it fed right into the back of the baby's head and was formed from the same papery material as the nest itself. And the baby . . .

"Oh," I breathed, and again, "oh . . ."

"He's turned out very well," the queen said proudly.

I took a big breath of the humid air, and strangely it didn't smell bad anymore. It smelled like a baby's milky breath.

"He's so beautiful," I said.

"Isn't he?"

He was all soft flesh and dimpled wrists and knees, and the most perfect bowed mouth. And I knew it was unmistakably our baby, before anything had gone wrong with its DNA, before it had come out of my mom's womb, before it slept in the crib in the bedroom down the hall from me.

"Can I touch him?" I asked.

"Not yet. We're not quite finished yet."

And when I looked more closely, I saw little teams of wasps moving over the baby's body—a little fingernail that wasn't quite complete, the lobe of an ear—and they were regurgitating matter from their mouths and sculpting it into baby flesh.

I watched these small construction sites, fascinated, and all the thoughts in my head, those hot prickly coils of static, somehow melted into a perfect quiet pool. I was so still inside.

"The pupal stage is quite comprehensive," the queen was saying, "but there's always a few last little bits to polish up. A few odds and ends. We like to take our time. Make sure it's just right before we put it into place." She called out to her workers: "Excellent work, ladies! Well done!"

The workers didn't seem to hear, or at least didn't make any reply. Maybe they couldn't talk.

"It's incredible," I said.

"Why, thank you. Some people don't appreciate how skilled we are. They can't see all the work that goes into it. They don't look closely enough, do they? I like to think of us as stonemasons. Like those workers who built the great cathedrals or pyramids. Thousands of them it took, and decades to complete sometimes."

The queen turned and called out cheerily to her workers again.

"Tremendous, ladies. Keep it up!"

Again they ignored her.

"Important to keep their spirits up," she confided to me. "They don't tend to get a lot of outside praise. Good for morale. Feel free to say something to them. It does buck them up so."

Awkwardly I called out, "Nice work, everyone!"

More quietly the queen said to me, "They don't live long, you know. A few weeks. But they have lots of energy. Their entire lives they give to this project. Just for you and your family. And look, there he is. Your little baby Theo. You can't tell me that's not him. Just without those unfortunate mistakes."

I remembered what Mom had said, about her dream, how they'd just made a mistake at the hospital. How they'd given her the wrong baby.

And then they'd brought her the right one.

"When I said yes, what does it mean? Exactly."

"Ah, well, I'm very glad you asked. When your baby is ready, we'll need to bring him into your house, into his crib."

"How will you do that?"

"You'll be helping us. That's what you said yes to. When we're finally ready, all you have to do is open the window in the baby's room and remove the screen. That's all. We'll do the rest. That's not so hard, is it? Just open the window and remove the screen. Open the window and remove the screen."

"Open the window, remove the screen," I repeated.

"Precisely."

"But what about our baby?" I asked.

"There you go again," the queen chastised.

"He's getting an operation soon . . . ," I said.

"Not going to happen," said the queen. "He's not going to live."

I swallowed. "You're sure?"

"I'm sure. And so are you. You've already made your choice, Steven. You can have your proper baby—or no baby at all. Which do you think is better for your family? It's not even a choice! A choice requires a bit of thought, a bit of a tussle. You didn't need to think about this at all. It's something or nothing. But we do need to give you the new baby before the old one dies."

I thought of all the agony Mom and Dad would endure if the baby died. I couldn't bear it, knowing I might have stopped it. Then I clenched my teeth, reminded myself I was only dreaming.

"None of this matters," I murmured.

The queen's head angled in surprise. "Doesn't matter?"

"This is just a dream. Just my mind."

"It's all right, Steven," she said. "I know this must be very difficult for you." She stroked me with her antennae, and I somehow felt forgiven. "Anyone would struggle with this. Would you like some help, knowing if this is real?"

I nodded.

"Of course you would. All right, then."

Very quickly she darted toward me and bit me. I cried out as the twin points of her mandibles pierced the back of my hand.

"I'm sorry," she said gently, "but now you'll know."

I cradled my hand, and the pain swelled to fill me up, then turned to blackness—and for the first time in a long time, I felt that things were going to be all right.

On the back of my right hand, in the morning's light, were two small red welts.

*A*T BREAKFAST I SAID TO DAD, "I FEEL SORT of bad about getting rid of the nest."

He looked up from buttering his toast. "You're kidding me."

After I'd woken up and seen the welts, I'd been scared I'd have an allergic reaction. But then I'd realized this was a bite, not a sting. No venom. I'd looked all over my bed for something with pointy edges I might have hit my hand on. Nothing. I knew how those marks had been made, but I couldn't tell Mom and Dad. They'd say there were lots of explanations for those marks. A spider or some other bug that had bitten me in the night. Knocking my hand on something without even noticing. I knew what they'd think.

But the queen had given me proof, just like she'd promised. My dreams were real. The nest was real. The baby they were making inside was real. But the exterminator was coming in two days, and what if the wasps couldn't finish the baby in time?

"I just started wondering if it was wrong," I said to Dad, trying to sound calm. "I mean, interfering with nature. They spent a long time making the nest and laying their eggs. And it's not like they're just pests. They pollinate flowers and plants."

"Uh-huh."

"They're an important part of the ecosystem."

"Has Vanessa been telling you all this?"

"No! Well, she told us some stuff about wasps,

but she's not saying we should keep the nest. I just . . . don't like the idea of killing so many of them, I guess. Just because of me."

Dad sighed and looked across the kitchen at Mom, who was busy with the coffeemaker. "Are you hearing this?"

"You're allergic, Steve," she said.

"I've got the EpiPen now. And I promise I won't freak out if they fly around me. Honestly, I'm not as scared of them anymore."

"That's great," Mom said, "but I still think it's a good idea."

"I've booked the guy; he's coming Friday," Dad said.

"I can cancel, if you want. What's the name of the company? I'll call."

Dad looked at me carefully, and I knew I'd gone too far, had sounded too urgent.

"Let's just leave it, okay?" Dad said. "I've got to get to work."

I nodded. "Sure."

After lunch Mom left for the hospital with the baby to meet the surgical team. Vanessa was over. I couldn't do it while Mom was home, but now I disappeared upstairs to search Mom and Dad's bedroom. There was an old green desk where they kept all their bills and other boring stuff, and I figured they might have written down the name of the exterminator.

There were tons of bits of paper, mostly stuff about the baby and doctors, and scribbled notes with times and addresses and phone numbers, but I couldn't find anything that looked like an exterminator. In one of the deep drawers I found a copy of the yellow pages, and when I lifted it out, I saw the knife.

Just the sight of it scared me. Its weird curve. But I couldn't stop myself from closing my fingers around the handle and feeling how good the grip was. The urge to stroke the blade, to feel its sharpness, was almost overwhelming. It could cut so much, so deep.

I took a breath and put it back into the drawer. I opened the yellow pages to "Pest Control." There was page after page, and none of the entries were circled or anything. It would take so long to call all of them. . . .

"Steven!"

It was Nicole's voice from downstairs.

"Where are you?" she shouted.

I slammed the yellow pages back into the drawer.

"Up here!"

"Phone call for you!"

The phone hadn't rung.

"Steven!"

"Yeah, okay, I'm coming!"

Nicole was waiting for me at the bottom of the stairs, holding out the receiver of her toy phone.

Vanessa grinned. "I think it's Mr. Nobody."

"He wants to talk to you," Nicole said.

I wasn't in the mood. "You talk to him, Nicole."

"He said he needs to talk to you."

This had never happened before. This was not part of the game. I didn't need any more weird stuff in my life. My weird little broken baby and my weird dreams and weird wasps. I didn't need a weirdo sister on top of it.

"Just shut up about Mr. Nobody, Nicole, all right! Nobody cares about Mr. Nobody."

She actually giggled. "That's funny," she said. "You just said 'Nobody cares about Mr. Nobody.' That means—"

"Shut up, Nicole!"

My little sister didn't say "Shut up" back. She just kept looking at me with her big brown eyes, holding out the plastic phone.

"Hey, Steven," Vanessa said. "Come on." She nodded toward the phone, urging me to just take it.

My feet didn't feel like they were touching the steps as I walked down. The phone was warm from Nicole's hand. I put it to my ear and felt angry and foolish at the same time. Silence.

"There's no one there," I said.

"You have to say hello," Nicole said solemnly. "Manners, Steven!"

It was just a stupid game, and I hadn't spent much time playing with Nicole lately, and I suddenly felt bad barking at her. "Oh, okay. Hello, Mr. Nobody. This is Steven." I looked at Nicole, and she seemed to want me to keep going. "How nice of you to call, Mr. Nobody. Yep, I'm very well, thanks. How are you?"

"Worried about you," said a voice in my ear.

It sounded like a piece of metal being held against a grindstone, shrill and raspy at the same time. It was like no human voice I'd ever heard. The phone was welded to my hand—I couldn't drop it. I swallowed wrong and started coughing.

"You'll need the knife," the voice said.

This time I jerked the phone away from my head. "What is this!" I shouted. "This is a stupid game, Nicole!"

"I told you," said Nicole, taking the phone from me and hanging up.

"Everything okay?" Vanessa asked. "Steve?"

I walked quickly to the bathroom and locked the door. I swayed in front of the toilet, trying to breathe, feeling my throat tighten and tighten, and

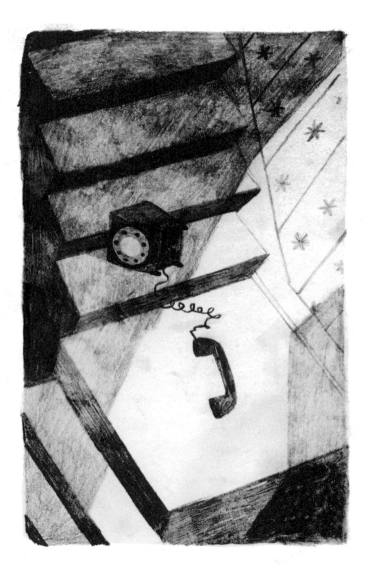

finally I hunched over and retched, but nothing came up. I retched a second and third time, spitting to clear the acid taste in my mouth.

Vanessa was knocking on the door. "You okay?"

Under the hot water I scrubbed and scrubbed my hands. I wanted to get the phone off me. Afterward I tried to pat them dry and not rub them with a towel, because that just chafed my skin, and if my mom saw my chafed hands, she would say something and be worried and look at Dad. I found some lotion in the medicine cabinet and slathered it on.

When I came out, Vanessa said, "You look kind of wrecked."

"Just an upset stomach. I get it sometimes. I'm fine. Don't tell Mom and Dad."

She didn't say anything.

"Vanessa, if you tell them, I'll tell Dad you told me more about the wasps. And he'll fire you."

She looked really hurt and shook her head, like she didn't understand why I was behaving like this.

"Fine. If you're sure," she said.

"I'm sure."

Later that afternoon Mom came back from the hospital, and she was smiling.

"They say he's doing much better," she said. "Much stronger now. They've scheduled him for Saturday morning."

All through dinner Dad and Mom and Nicole were happy, and I was keeping a smile glued to my face. I felt like my head was going to explode off my shoulders. I had no idea what to think anymore. I'd heard voices on a toy telephone. The baby was getting stronger, not weaker like the queen had told me. She'd said he would never be well enough for surgery. Either she was lying or the doctors were. But I couldn't tell Mom and Dad any of this, because if I did, they'd take me right down to Emergency and I'd be admitted and pumped full of drugs, and then I wouldn't be able to do anything about the baby.

I felt shattered and all in pieces.

Nicole still liked me to help tuck her in, so after Mom and Dad said good night, it was my turn.

"Hey," I whispered, kneeling beside her bed, "how long have you been talking to Mr. Nobody?"

She frowned. "Not so long. You heard him, right?"

"He really talks to you?" I said. "Like I'm talking to you right now?"

She nodded.

"It's not pretend?"

Scornfully she said, "I know what pretend is."

"Okay." I felt a little better. Either my sister was crazy too or neither of us were.

"What does Mr. Nobody tell you?"

"Mostly just stuff like, 'Be safe. Watch out for the wasps. Take care of your little brother. Make sure your big brother is all right.'"

I blinked. "Really?"

"Mm-hmm. So, are you all right?"

I almost laughed. "I guess so. Who is he?"

Nicole shrugged.

"Can you call him?"

She shook her head. "I tried. He only calls me."

"But the phone never rings."

"I hear it."

"No one else does."

Nicole didn't seem bothered by this. "It's a special ring. You guys just aren't listening."

"Does he talk about the wasps?"

"He says they can really hurt the baby. But you'll take care of him."

She snuggled down deeper into her bed. "Tuck me in now."

I pulled the blankets up around her shoulders and chin.

"My nest," she said happily.

*I*N THE NEST IT WAS VERY DARK, AND THE smell hit me at once—a barnyard stench, chicken droppings and pig manure. And I was aware of the baby above me, crowding against the walls. I didn't want to look.

"Ah, there you are," said the queen. "It's so exciting. He's almost ready. Look!"

Reluctantly I looked. Somehow the baby had turned in its nest and was upside down, bum near the ceiling and its bald head closest to me.

The moment I saw its face, the chicken coop smell disappeared and a beautiful fragrance filled the nest: Theo's head after his bath, a smell so intense, you wanted to kiss that head again and again.

"You're doing something," I said to the queen. "Changing the smells. Something to do with pheromones."

"Pheromones! That's a big word. Well done. Who's been telling you about pheromones?"

"Vanessa." Immediately I regretted saying her name. I didn't like the wasps knowing about people in my life.

"She's a clever one. But we all produce pheromones. How do you know they're not your own? Triggered by the baby, telling you to love him and care for him."

Such a perfect head and nose he had, and full

molded lips. And already such long beautiful eyelashes.

"You seem agitated, Steven," the queen said.
She touched my face. "Tell me your troubles."

"I got a phone call."

"I'm not at all surprised," she replied calmly. "I
expected him sooner."

"You know who he is?"

"He's one of many. He's nothing and darkness.
He's a troublemaker who doesn't like our work."

"He said—"

"He's a liar. And he's not your friend, Steven.
He's your nightmare. He's a lingerer who stands
and watches at the foot of children's beds."

A quick flare of terror went through my body.
"Maybe, yes . . ."

"Absolutely. Anything else troubling you?"

"He's much better," I told the queen.

"Sorry? Who?"

"Our baby. Theo."

"I don't think so."

"He's scheduled for surgery on Saturday. He's strong enough!"

"Well, it doesn't matter one way or another."

I shook my head. "But you said he was going to die before then!"

"We can't know everything, Steven."

I looked around the nest, at the beautiful baby on the stalk. I looked at my feet, thought about Theo in his crib, getting healthier.

I said, "I've changed my mind, then."

The queen was silent, regarding me with her huge compound eyes. "Excuse me?"

"When I said yes—I take it back."

She just watched me.

"I made a mistake," I told her.

"Once you say yes, you can't say no."

"Well, it was just a mistake."

She sounded exasperated. "Once you say yes, you can't say no!"

"Who says?"

"That's just the way it is."

"Who makes these rules?"

"Ha! Not me!"

"Who, then?"

The queen twitched her antennae irritably.

"Who?" I demanded.

"You're shouting."

"You lied to me! You said the baby would die and this would be the only way we could have the baby!"

"You're shouting again, Steven. You're upset. Deep breaths, come on, just like Dr. Brown taught you. A big balloon in your tummy. Fill that balloon up."

"The baby might not die!"

"We're quibbling," said the queen. "Let's say the baby survives this operation, which frankly is a big 'if,' if you want my expert and honest opinion. Now, say he survives. So what?"

"What do you mean?"

"His defective heart is just the beginning. Tip of the iceberg. Life is going to be very difficult for him. There will be suffering for him and for the whole family. You think it'll be fun having a freaky little brother in your house? This is the truth I'm telling you. Maybe you won't like your freaky little brother. Maybe your friends won't. Maybe they won't come over."

My friends didn't come over much anyway. I didn't have a ton of friends.

"It might not walk. It might not talk. It might not be able to feed itself. It might not think properly. It might never know how to go to the toilet. You'll be cleaning up its pee and poo your whole life."

"You don't know that!"

"Oh, forgive me, you do?"

"No. No one does. We have to—"

"Wait and see, oh I know. Wait and see. What's the point? When you can have everything fixed right now? Who would turn down a gift like that? Are you the Grinch or something?"

At that moment the baby opened its eyes and looked at me. The look was so frank and clear, it was impossible not to gaze back.

"Perfect, isn't he?" said the queen.

"Is he?" I asked, slightly dazed by the baby's beauty.

"Of course. What would be the point otherwise? Why go to all this trouble?"

"No one's perfect," I said, but I wasn't certain anymore.

"Oh ho!" The queen's antennae twitched, and the whiskers around her face glittered as they caught the light. "That's where you're wrong. That's the old way of thinking. I've been at this a long time, and some of my babies have really made a difference. Leaders and visionaries who have done remarkable things. At the risk of sounding boastful, I'd say some of my babies have gone on to change the world. But this one is my best yet. My masterpiece, I think. And that's what we're offering you. This perfect baby."

"But what about ours?" I asked.

"Oh, I see. You think we're heartless?"

She was turning restlessly from side to side, and I caught a glimpse of her abdomen and at the very end of it, the stinger, the sharpest and thinnest of thorns. At the tip welled a small drop of venom.

"You think we're cruel and heartless? But who

wouldn't want a perfectly healthy child? And a very, very clever one, I might add! The IQ of this one here is going to be off the charts! A baby who won't get sick. And won't be anxious. And won't feel lonely and depressed. Someone who's fearless! And courageous! Someone who can make the world a better place! That's what we're giving you. It's Christmas come early! It's what every parent wants. It's what everyone wants. Just look at him. Steven, you're not even looking at him!"

"I don't want to look at him!"

"How can you say that?" she asked with such genuine sorrow that I felt ashamed. "You've heard him cry. You've seen his eyelashes. He has you inside him."

With a sick shock I remembered how the queen had stung me and taken some of my DNA for the new baby. I looked up at his eyes, so calm and serene. All my thoughts started to fray and spark, like the burning end of a fuse.

"Are you saying you don't want him to be born?" the queen asked. "He's your own brother. He wants to be born."

"Let him be born!" I shouted above the noise inside my head. "But why does Theo have to get replaced? It's not fair! Just give this one to someone else! They can both live!"

The queen's abdomen twitched. "Don't be absurd. You think we can just leave him on someone's doorstep in a wicker basket? This baby is meant only for you and your family. And, Steven, you're forgetting the most important thing. There is only one baby."

"There are two!"

"There is one, and only one will live."

"I didn't want any of this!" I yelled in fury. "None of it!" I was suddenly sobbing, tears and snot all over my face. "It's not fair! I didn't want this. I didn't ask for this!"

"Of course not," she said, stroking my face. "Of course you didn't. But here we are, and things would be so much better if you were at least honest with yourself, Steven."

I stepped away from her. "What do you mean?"

"Do you really like being afraid so much? All your nightmares. All your lists and worries and compulsions. Is that fun, Steven? I don't think so. Do you? Imagine if we could have helped you."

"You mean replaced me!"

"Oh dear, oh dear, it always comes back to these silly terms you use. Wouldn't it be nice to be normal and sleep without hiding under the covers and wishing you could disappear into the floor?"

"I don't do that anymore," I lied. I hated how she knew so much about me. I felt invaded.

"I know all about you, all your little bits and pieces, from when I stung you. We could still help you, you know. Your case isn't so severe. We can make little adjustments."

"Adjustments . . ."

"A few little tweaks and twokes. To help you be more of who you are, make you who you really want to be. All you have to do is help us."

I felt my chest ache at the thought. Normal. More of who I wanted to be.

"You could do that?" I asked.

"Absolutely." She stroked my face. I let her.

"I open the window and the screen and you come in. . . ."

"Yes, we'll come in and we'll be carrying your baby very gently. It'll take a lot of us, but we're very strong, surprisingly strong when we all fly together. We can carry a lot."

I remembered the wasp I'd seen on the outdoor table, hefting the enormous dead spider.

"We'll place the baby in his crib, and we'll tuck him up, and there he'll be."

"And then what?" I asked.

I needed to know everything. Every step. I looked up again at the baby's open eyes. There was something else in them that I couldn't name. It wasn't innocence. This baby wasn't waiting to learn right or wrong, good or bad, love or hate. It already knew. It already had the answers to everything. There was nothing that was weak about this baby, there was nothing this baby would suffer.

"We'll put Theo in his crib," the queen was saying. "And then I'll give him a little sting—sort of like a smack on the bottom to get him breathing, to bring him properly to life."

"And the other baby?"

"What other baby?" the queen asked.

"Stop doing that! Theo . . . the one already there! Theo now in his crib!"

"When we leave, we'll take the broken parts away with us."

"Broken parts?"

"Well, why would you want to keep them? It's just clutter. We always clean up after ourselves. Haven't you had workers in your house fixing something and they leave all their mess behind? Terrible. Debris and bits and pieces they didn't use. That's not how we operate. We leave everything just as we found it, only much, much better."

"No, it's not—it's not right." I stepped back from the queen's antenna, but it snaked after me. "You can't just take away our baby like he's trash. It's not right."

"It's not like we don't put it to good use," she said indignantly.

"What do you mean?"

"We take it back to the nest."

For a moment I was hopeful. Stupidly I said, "And take care of it?"

"No, no. The workers eat it. They've been working like slaves, haven't they? You've seen how hard they work! They need their reward. It's only fair. Quite a feast it makes."

The baby smiled down at me. Maybe it was just a gas grimace, or maybe it was having a dream of glory before its birth. But I knew, absolutely I knew, that this perfect baby didn't care about our little Theo. It didn't care about me or anyone else. It couldn't, because it was so perfect that it wouldn't even understand what it was like not to be perfect. It could never know weakness or fear.

But I could. Because I was broken inside too. And in that instant I decided that this perfect baby would never replace my brother.

I said, "I won't help anymore."

"Oh, for heaven's sakes. We have a contract."

"I didn't sign anything!"

"You don't need to. A spoken yes is still a contract. And we honor our contracts, don't we? Or where would we be? People saying yes when they meant no, and no when they meant yes? That's no way of running a society. And we want a good orderly society. That's why we make our babies so perfect. Only a perfect baby can make a perfect society."

"I'm not helping!" I shouted. "I—do—not—say—yes!"

I expected her to be angry and show me her stinger again, to squeeze out a larger drop of venom. Why hadn't she stung me earlier? The only answer I could think was that she needed me. Just like she'd said, they couldn't do this without me.

"Steven. If you don't help, he'll die."

"No! If I help, our baby will die!"

"This baby is your baby. Why can't you see that? This is your baby, only healthy, only without flaw and blemish! This is our gift to you! You're hyperventilating, Steven. Remember, deep breaths, just like Dr. Brown told you."

"I'll tell my parents!"

"Oh! Good heavens, such an idea! Please go right ahead. I can tell you exactly what will happen. They'll send you straight to the psychiatric ward for assessment and pump you full of sedatives and antipsychotics and start debating your diagnosis. Maybe schizophrenia, bipolar disorder, or who knows what other concoction they'll invent for you!"

I knew she was right. I had to keep it all locked up in myself, spun and sealed like in a cocoon.

"Now," the queen said, "tomorrow is Thursday, and we'll be calling on you then. Be ready."

*T*HURSDAY AFTERNOON DAD WAS AT WORK, AND Mom was out at some kind of parental support group. Vanessa was walking Nicole to a birthday party and then doing some errands before picking her up and bringing her back. I was alone in the house with the baby.

I knew that whatever the wasps were going to do, it would be at night and I had to be ready. Theo was taking his nap, and I was downstairs in the kitchen with the baby monitor on. I got a pen and piece of paper—and stared at it, trying to form a plan, trying to think of a list of things that might help, that I might need.

Over the baby monitor a voice said: "Steven."

My breathing stopped, the air corked in my throat. It was her voice, the queen's. This wasn't right; it wasn't nighttime. I wasn't dreaming yet. I forced a breath into my lungs.

"Steven."

I changed the channel on the monitor. There was a flare of static and then:

"It's time, Steven. Open the baby's window and remove the screen."

"No."

I didn't even know if she could hear me through the receiver, but she said:

"You agreed, Steven."

"I changed my mind. I told you! How many times do I have to tell you!"

"Steven, I really must insist that you open the window for us. The baby's ready. You wouldn't want to hurt the baby."

Theo. I grabbed the monitor and bolted upstairs to his room.

"There's a good boy," the queen said over the monitor. "It'll all turn out right. You'll see. And we can help you, too, just like I promised. You'll be so much better. No more lists and prayers and hand-washing and fears."

Theo was sleeping peacefully in his crib. I walked to the window, raised the blind—and with a gasp let it drop. Beyond the glass was a swarm of pale wasps, as thick as mist. I could hear the faint thrum of their wings.

"Steven. All you need to do is open the window now. We're ready to bring your baby inside."

I wasn't ready. My thoughts were sharp, useless

little shards of glass. I pulled in a breath, one more.

I ran. From room to room upstairs, I checked every window was shut tight. I hammered downstairs and did the same thing. We'd had the air-conditioning on for a week solid, so all the windows were already shut, but wherever I could, I pushed the sashes down harder or cranked the handles tighter.

I raced back up to the baby's room to check on Theo. He was still sleeping soundly. Beyond the window I heard a slow scratching. Parting the blinds, I saw the windowsill and frame carpeted with wasps, their mandibles working at the wood. One little scrape after another. They were being very methodical. One would chew off a strip, then step aside so a fellow wasp could take her place and scrape away along the same gash, making it deeper and wider.

"We can chew our way in, Steven," came the queen's voice over the baby monitor.

"It'll take forever," I said. There was the window to get through, and then the mesh screen.

"There are so many of us."

I ran to my room and pulled on my jeans and thickest socks. I laced tight my high-top sneakers. I pulled on a sweatshirt and a hoodie. After grabbing my knapsack, I belted downstairs to the basement. My eyes flew over the cluttered, dusty shelf where we kept all our old paint and chemicals and junk. I grabbed two cans of Raid and a flyswatter. In soggy boxes and plastic bins, I found some old swimming goggles, a pair of flowered gardening gloves, and two rolls of duct tape, and I threw it all into the knapsack. From the ground-floor medicine cabinet I took my EpiPen and zipped it into my bag too. I slung the pack over both shoulders and cinched it tight.

Outside each window I passed, I saw the pale tracery of the wasps. If I paused for even a second, the pattern would thicken into a darker mass, like wisps of storm cloud. How could there be so many? Were they just following me from window to window, or were there really millions of them, enveloping the entire house?

I wondered if I could bundle the baby into a blanket, bolt out of the house, and go to one of the neighbors. Would the wasps follow me? I peeked out the tall skinny window beside the front door. They were already there. The moment I opened the door, they'd be all over us. They'd sting me and sting me, and then the baby—and lift it away to their nest and eat it.

I checked the back door. Same thing.

Running upstairs to the baby's room. From outside the window:

Scritch, scratch, scritch.

The familiar hot flush of panic coursed through me. I wasn't thinking very well. Someone would see, wouldn't they? Outside, someone would see all these swarming wasps and call the police or something. But maybe their bodies were so pale you couldn't see them from the street, from a passing car.

I grabbed the hall phone, dialed 911. I got a voice menu with a lot of choices. Ambulance? Police? Fire department? I chose fire department and had to wait for a bit. When the operator answered, I started gabbling.

"There's wasps outside my house, a ton of them, and they're trying to get in."

"You say you've got a wasps' nest outside your house?"

"Thousands of them, and they're swarming all

round the windows and they're trying to get inside. We've got a baby, and—"

With every word I knew how crazy it sounded.

"Sir, this number is for emergencies only. It sounds like you need to call an exterminator."

"You don't understand—" And the line went dead. At first I thought she'd hung up on me. But when I tried to call again, there was no dial tone. The wasps had chewed through our phone line.

Back to the baby's room to check on him—*scritch, scratch, scritch*—then I raced to my own room and grabbed my cell. The battery was dead. I started tossing stuff all over the place, searching for my charger—and saw a single wasp on my wall.

Quietly I sat on the bed and watched. It was just one wasp. But how had it gotten inside? Slowly I shrugged the knapsack off my right shoulder, unzipped it just enough to reach in and pull out the flyswatter. The wasp wasn't very high up. I walked swiftly toward it and whacked the heck out of it. Three, four smashes, and it fell. I stamped on it with my heel and felt it crack.

When I ran out of my room, I saw three more wasps on our big air-conditioning unit. That was how they were getting in. Somehow they were flying through the whirling blades of the outside fan unit without getting chopped into bits, crawling up the hose and then out through the slats of the hall unit. I grabbed the Raid and blasted them. Coated with white foam, they dropped off the wall so I could crush them.

I turned the power off on the air conditioner, and the slats automatically angled shut, but not before a couple more wasps slipped inside. I swatted them, then duct taped over all the slats. That was good. We were safer now. We were airtight.

In the baby's room—*scritch, scratch, scritch, sca-raaaatch*. But none had gotten through yet; there were still no wasps on the walls or ceiling. Careening downstairs to the coatrack, I found the cloth baby carrier thing. I ran back up, trying to put it on. It was complicated and took me a while to get the straps figured out with the knapsack in the way.

Carefully I lifted Theo from his crib and slid him against my chest into the carrier. It was tricky to get his floppy legs into the right slots, and then his arms. He woke up a little and started to murmur, but I shushed him and rocked up and down on my heels. Hummed some of the songs Mom used to sing to me. He settled back into sleep, his wet little mouth parted like it was awaiting food.

I tightened all the straps and the neck support so his head was nice and snug and wouldn't loll around. He needed to be with me now. I couldn't keep leaving him alone, even for a second.

Without the air-conditioning, the house was heating up. But I liked Theo's weight against me, his heat. It made me feel less alone. He was part of me, and I felt stronger somehow. Vanessa would be back soon, or my parents, and they'd see the wasps swarming outside and they'd call and get help.

Scritch, scratch, scritch, scaaaa-raaaatch.

I parted the blinds. My stomach swirled. Outside, wasps teemed against the glass and wooden frame, three or four deep. It looked like chaos, but quickly I saw how hard they were working. In some places they'd gouged their way so deeply into the wood that you could see only the back half of their bodies.

"Steven," said the queen over the monitor, and I jerked. I'd forgotten about her. "This really is awfully inconvenient for us. And unfortunate, too.

We could still turn this around if you'd just be reasonable."

Baby against my chest, knapsack against my back, I went downstairs to check the windows again. Same as last time—within seconds of my appearance, there was a dark vapor of wasps swirling, waiting.

I kept moving, my eyes sweeping the walls and ceilings, keeping watch. When I got back to the upstairs hallway, I froze. There were four, five, six wasps on the ceiling, not moving. From the spare bedroom a seventh appeared, crawling over the top of the door to join the others.

There must have been another hole somewhere, some way they were getting inside. Where? The windows were all shut tight. How, then?

The wasps were too high for me to get with the swatter, so I reached into the little gap I'd left open in the knapsack and pulled out the Raid. I reached high and blasted them. They didn't even try to fly away. They were just stupid worker drones. But after I'd trampled them for good measure, heard their bodies crack, I realized I was using up too much Raid. There were thousands, and I had only two cans.

I fought back my panic with little sentences.

Be more careful.

Use the flyswatter whenever you can.

Raid is only a last resort.

They were coming from the spare room. Cautiously I stepped in and saw another wasp emerge from the walk-in closet. This one I got with the swatter. I pushed the closet door wide and took a few paces inside. I pulled the chain on the hanging lightbulb. On either side of the closet were rows of clothes, and underneath, bins with winter things. In the center of the ceiling was a hatch. I'd never thought of our house as having an attic. Really it was just a crawl space. A few years ago some guys had gone up there to blow in some insulation.

I stood very still for a bit. I couldn't hear anything. But I didn't like the look of that hatch. It didn't look snug. Wasps must have been crawling through the gaps. On the floor by the shoes was a plastic footstool, but it wasn't high enough to get me up to the hatch. I left the closet and brought back a chair. I took out my duct tape.

Standing on the chair, I laid a strip down along the first side of the hatch. It jiggled. It really wasn't tight-fitting at all. As I taped down the second side, I pushed too hard, and the hatch popped up and turned a bit so it wouldn't slip properly back into place. I reached up with my fingers and tried hurriedly to jiggle it around, but it was tricky, with the baby, and my knapsack and my careening heart.

To get a good grip I had to push the hatch up even more—and the harsh light from the bare bulb blared right up into the crawl space. A flash of dark rafters, and bits of paper and foam insulation coating the floor, and off to the right something so out of place, it took me a second to understand what I was looking at.

It was like a mountain of gray animal excrement. It rose from the timbered floor into a series of sloppy peaks that fused to the rafters. All across the papery dead surface of this vast nest were pale wasps. Thousands of them, motionless, not making a sound. I jerked backward so fast, I nearly fell off the chair. I knocked the lightbulb so it swung crazily, throwing light then dark into the attic, light and dark, and that was when the sound started— the terrible buzzing, so angry and loud that it plowed almost every thought from my head.

Run. That was all I wanted to do. But I made one last try to drag the hatch back into place. It wasn't right, it wasn't snug, but I was slamming down strips of duct tape any which way, ripping them off with my teeth, all these ragged pieces across the hatch and ceiling, trying to seal it up.

It wasn't good enough. The wasps started coming through the gaps, and I was afraid for myself and Theo. I jumped off the chair, cupping his head with one hand—and dropped my roll of duct tape. No time to grab it, too many wasps swarming, so I just backed out of the closet and slammed the door shut. I dragged the blanket off the bed and jammed it under the door. Already I could see the wasps crawling out through the side jambs and over the top.

In the hall I shut the door to the spare room and shrugged off my knapsack. I yanked out the last roll of duct tape.

"Did you think there was just one nest?" the queen asked, loud and clear, from the monitor in the baby's room. "Where did you think all my workers were birthed? It takes a lot of workers to build a nest and feed a baby. And such a big baby too."

I was already rolling out a line of tape along the bottom of the door, but it wasn't sticking very well to the carpet. I felt sick, just thinking of the shape and sheer size of the nest, like something oozed out from an evil ice cream machine, wave after wave of goo, congealing on the floor and producing little larvae and pupae and wasps.

From the monitor came the sound of a baby wailing and crying, wanting to be born.

"It's going to be okay," I said, touching Theo's sleeping head.

I started duct taping the left side of the door,

but only got halfway before a spurt of wasps flew out at me through the gaps. I fell back. With my free hand I grabbed the can of Raid and let fly. I sprayed the whole lot of them, hard and long, so that they fell out of the air like they were coated in cement.

Hurriedly I put the swimming goggles over my eyes and pulled the drawstrings of my hood tight. I made sure my jeans went over the rims of my high-tops. The gardening gloves made my fingers feel a bit clumsy, but I could still work the spray nozzle.

"Sorry, Theo," I said after blasting a second wave of wasps. I felt bad that his little lungs had to breathe in the spray. But I had no choice. I didn't dare put him down anywhere I couldn't see him.

From Nicole's room I heard a phone ringing and thought I must be imagining it. The phone line was dead. The wasps had chewed through it.

But when it rang again, I knew this was a sound I'd never heard in our house before. It was shriller, more like an old-fashioned alarm clock with a hammer that beat at two little bells. Nicole's toy phone.

Triiiiing-triiiiing! Triiing-triiiiing!

I had an overpowering urge to answer it but was worried that if I broke off from the door, too many wasps would get through and overwhelm me. I kept taping and spraying, but it wasn't doing much good. There were too many wasps now, and they kept coming. The nozzle of my can started to spit and fizzle. On the other side of the spare room door, the buzzing mounted—like the sound cicadas make at the end of summer before they die, the sound of high voltage and heat and death.

Triiiiing-triiiiing! Triiing-a-liiing-a-liiing!

"Don't answer that, Steven," said the queen from the monitor.

That was all I needed to hear. With a final blast of Raid, I dropped the empty can and bolted into Nicole's room. I saw the plastic phone, snatched up the receiver.

"The knife," said the voice like a grindstone.

"The knife?"

"Use it," the metal voice scraped out.

"How's a knife going to help me?" I shouted.

"Get a grip."

"Hey, wait!" I said, but there was nothing more.

It didn't matter. I knew exactly what he was talking about. I was already rushing to my parents' room. I yanked open the drawer, dragged out the yellow pages, and took hold of the knife. My grip was good.

When I turned, there was a cloud of wasps in front of me. On instinct I slashed at them with the knife, cutting the air stroke after stroke, not knowing if it was doing one bit of good, until I saw the wasps' severed bodies raining down on my shoes. The knife had been made for my hand. It was like a scythe of impossible sharpness, and I whirled left and right, cutting back and forth in a zigzag until there was not a single wasp left in the air before me. I was panting and sweating and triumphant.

"Come on, then!" I shouted. "Hah! See? See? Come on!"

With my free hand I reached around into my knapsack and grabbed my last can of Raid. I popped the top off, then strutted back down the hallway, knife raised, toward the spare room door, where another wave of wasps was gathering—and then I stopped.

From Theo's room, at the very end of the hall, came a rattling sound. I had a clear view of the window and saw the closed blind bulge as if pushed by a gust of wind, then knock back against the screen.

With a *pop*, the blind bucked like it had been kicked from the outside. The screen clattered to the floor, and the wasps came. They came in a gray torrent around the edges of the blind and then right through it, their mandibles obliterating it into confetti.

I knew, even with my knife, there was no way I could fend them all off like this, coming at me now from two directions. I ran into my parents' bathroom, slammed the door, and locked it. I put the knife down in the sink and got to work. Along the bottom of the door, the duct tape stuck well to the tiles, way better than to the hall carpeting.

I moved on to the left side of the door. Done. Good. Right side. Done. Good. Across the top. Harder, nothing to stand on to reach it properly. But done. I had a single layer down on all sides now, and nothing was coming through yet. I didn't stop. I laid down a second layer, then a third. Good. Still nothing. I held my breath a moment and heard only silence from the other side.

"You and me are going to be just fine," I said to Theo.

I looked all around the bathroom, saw the fan vent. Standing on the toilet, I put three layers of duct tape over it. I was sweating pretty hard now, could feel little rivers flowing down my flanks from my armpits. My heart furnaced away, heating up the bathroom even more.

There were white venetian blinds over the window, and when I parted two of the slats, it was like peering into fog. A wall of wasps was swarming outside, and I could barely see the trees and rooftops through their translucent bodies.

I started taping around the window frame, and then right across the screen too, until it was entirely covered.

By now I was feeling pretty wobbly, and I sat down on the edge of the bathtub and stroked the baby's head and made shushing noises, even though he was still fast asleep. A good sleeper, our Theo. I opened up my knapsack and spread out all my gear within easy reach. The one good can of Raid. Flyswatter. The last roll of duct tape, getting skinny. I wished I had some energy bars. My hands shook. I went to the sink and got the knife. Just holding it made me feel better.

I drank some water from the tap. I taped over the drain hole, just in case. I watched the bottom of the door to make sure nothing was coming through. I just had to wait now. Wait for someone to come home—or at least see the house covered in wasps and call someone. Would it be the police? The ambulance? The firemen to spray down the house with a hose? But who could really stop them, these wasps? This thought made my heart beat even harder. Who could clear them away in time?

Dry scratching from all around the door. I put down more tape. I hoped it would slow them. Surely their legs would get stuck to the sticky side and make it harder for their mandibles to chew through. Wouldn't it?

A distinct smell filled the house now—and it wasn't my body's smell, or the baby needing a change. It was a smell I recognized from my dreams in the nest. A pheromone. A wasp smell that the queen must have used to communicate with all her workers. I wondered if she was actually inside now, ordering them with her scent.

I rested my EpiPen on the edge of the sink. The doctor had showed me how to use it. Jab it into a bare leg, but in a pinch, any skin would do. I wondered how many wasp stings it was good for.

Rattling in the fan vent. I laid down another layer of tape. Standing on the toilet, I could see the tape pucker with the weight of their muscular little bodies—and then a pair of tiny mandibles cut through. I taped over the hole fast.

Outside the window the noise grew to a kind of frenzied growl. It was the sound of wood being pulped. I tried to figure out where the noise was loudest, and stretched the last of my duct tape there. I was out.

"Don't worry," I said to the baby. "We're going to be okay."

Back to the wall, I stood, knife in one hand, last can of Raid in the other.

I waited. I put a small towel over the baby's head, adjusted it so it wasn't covering his nose or mouth, so he could still breathe okay.

I saw the tape across the bottom of the door start to move, saw a head poke through, then another.

I kicked at them until there were too many getting through. Then I stepped back and adjusted my grip on the knife.

I cut them down as they came, the knife so unbelievably thin and sharp, slitting the air and the wasps with it. But it was different this time, I could tell right away. There were more of them, and they pushed harder.

I sprayed out a thick wall of Raid and fell back, then started slashing again in all directions, scything them down. They were coming in a thick gray torrent from the fan vent now too. I let fly with more Raid. In huge waves they came at me, and I blasted away until the air was foggy and I was coughing and retching. I worried the baby would suffocate.

The screen went, and the wasps poured through the window. I backed myself up into a corner. Even through the spray they kept coming, and then there was nothing left in the can.

Back and forth I cut with the knife, but there were just too many now.

The wasps were on my clothing, against the swimming goggles. My hoodie was cinched tight around my face, but I could feel them on the fabric, trying to get underneath. I swatted them on my body and away from the baby, who was awake now, because I had to swat him on his little head too when the wasps landed there.

I felt the first sting on my ankle. They'd gotten up under my jeans. Then a second on my temple. They were inside my hoodie. I kept slashing with the knife, just trying to keep them away from the baby and myself. It was no good. Pain seared my right wrist and hand—so intense that I dropped the knife. I saw it hit the floor, and then I couldn't see it anymore, because the wasps were all over it.

Another sting. They were trying to kill me this time. They didn't need me anymore. All they needed was the baby. My left eye was swelling shut. Another hot stab in my cheek. I lurched over to the sink, grabbed my EpiPen, and pulled off my glove. In the time it took to jab myself in the soft part of my wrist, I must have gotten stung six more times.

My heart surged, like pots banging in my chest. I was stamping on the wasps, slamming my back against them to crush them against the walls. Smashing them with my swollen fists. Doing a maniacal death dance in the fog. If I could just see the knife . . .

I couldn't catch my breath. My face felt fat. I could barely see through the goggles. More stings came, and more.

It was no good, no good. I was all stung and broken, and there were too many of them. I staggered into the bathtub and pulled the shower curtain shut—as if that would do anything, as if it would stop them for even one second. I crouched down in the tub and covered the baby with my body. I tried to seal him safely under me, my arms and legs all folded up tight so nothing could get to him. Like he was all tucked up in bed, and the floor could open and he could slide down and a door would close over him and nothing could get him. He was safe.

I felt them all over me, my back and my neck. They found ways in. And I just tried to keep my body tight and hard like a turtle shell over the baby.

I thought I heard a sound beyond the bathroom door, not a buzzing or a scraping but the peal of a handbell. And then there was another terrible noise—and I realized it was me, rasping for breath, like trying to suck air through a straw.

And then my heart swelled up like a big balloon of darkness.

SLOWLY I WOKE, SURROUNDED BY SOFT WALLS, close on both sides and low overhead. It was like being wrapped up in bed with a duvet pulled over my head. I exhaled and felt warm and safe. I was still folded up, my arms and legs beneath me, head bowed. Like a baby in the womb.

The baby.

I realized Theo wasn't with me. I felt for him with my hand. I was more awake now. I managed to flip over onto my back. There was just enough room to do that, the ceiling was so low, the walls so close. There was a give to them, but when I pushed harder and tried to dig in with my fingernails, they were surprisingly strong. It was very dim, just the grayest of light, and when I looked down to my feet, I saw a hexagonal opening, and taking up almost all of that opening was the queen's head.

From her mandibles glistened a thick paste as she laid down layer after layer, sealing me inside the cell.

"Hey!" I shouted, and tried to kick at her half-built wall.

Swiftly she swiveled and jabbed her long stinger into the cell, dripping venom. I backed up fast. She continued with her work.

"Where's the baby?" I shouted.

One of her long antennae snaked into the cell and touched my foot.

"The baby's fine. He's ready to be born."

"I mean my baby—not your baby!"

"Don't you see how ridiculous this whole argument is?" she said, still working away swiftly. "And tiring. You must be so tired, Steven. You're fighting a losing battle. People lie and say they don't want perfect. But really they do. Perfect bodies and minds and comfy chairs and cars and vacations and boyfriends and girlfriends and pets and children. Above all, children. Why do we lie and say we don't? Because we're afraid people will think we're mean or vain or cruel. But we all want it. Me, I'm just helping it come true. I'm at least telling the truth. No liars here, no sir."

"Let me out!"

"Just calm down and take a breath and stop trying. Stop fighting."

"Don't hurt Theo!"

"I'd love to accommodate you. Really I would.

But things have been set in motion. People have said yes. Agreements have been made. There are procedures to be followed."

"I'm going to stop you! I'm going to destroy your nest!"

"Oh my goodness, that will be difficult. Since you're dead."

Instantly I felt like my chest was collapsing, like it was made from the paper of the nest and it was all crumbling inward. "What?"

"No one likes being the bearer of bad news. Gosh, you look really upset. Come on, now, don't take it so hard. Actually, you know what? You're not quite dead yet. Unconscious certainly, but I can still hear a pulse. The pitter-patter of tiny beats. Rather irregular. I wouldn't give you long. You've been stung a lot. Breathe, remember. Deep breaths! Come on now."

"I'm not dying!" I shouted, feeling suddenly cold all through. Yet, like an echo through my limbs— or was it just a memory?—I felt my heart pumping faintly and erratically.

All the while, the queen was still building her wall, and there was only a little bit of her face showing now, her eyes and antennae.

"But you can still be useful to us, Steven," she said. "Don't you worry. Once the baby was finished, there was really just one last thing for me to do. Do you know what that was?"

"No," I wheezed.

"Lay one last egg. Make a new queen."

She pulled back her antenna, and I caught a final glimpse of her busy mandibles before the hole was sealed over.

I kicked and shouted at the hexagonal wall.

"Let me out! Where's Theo? Theo!"

But nothing gave. They were master builders, these wasps, and whatever I was now, alive or dead, I didn't have the strength to break through my cell. Maybe I had already gone and died, because I felt so tired, though in a nice way. Like after a summer day spent bicycling or hiking and all your limbs were pleasantly sore and heavy.

Behind my head the cell wall moved. I reached back with a hand, pushed, and felt something shift a bit. With a surge of hope I clumsily flipped myself onto my stomach. With both hands I pushed. They went through up to the wrists, into a thick goo. Grunting in disgust, I pulled back and squinted at the wall. It wasn't a wall but a large sac I'd just punctured. Ooze seeped out. Within was something shapeless and white, and as big as me. Its two black dot eyes were fixed on me, and below them was a big hole of a mouth, rimmed with barbs.

I cried out and pushed myself back, but there was really nowhere to go. The cell was so small. My feet drummed against the queen's new wall, but it held. She'd sealed me inside with her egg, and now it had hatched and I was going to be the larva's first food.

Slowly it was wriggling out of its sac, moving its pasty grub-like body closer to me. I punched its face, and it flinched but then inched forward again, its big mouth wide, hungry for its food.

From behind me came a loud ripping. I wrenched my head round and saw something sharp pierce the hexagonal wall and cut a slash from one end to the other. I felt a push against my head and gave a shout. Turning back, I recoiled, and saw the larva's moist face pressed against mine, its mouth trying to fit itself around my skull. I squeezed myself farther back, as small as I could, and then heard a second ripping sound near my feet.

Two diagonal slashes in the wall made a jagged X. A dark shape thrust right through the center and started cracking the wall apart, piece by piece.

"Help!" I shouted—at whatever it was that wanted to come in.

I felt the larva's barbed teeth start to test their grip on my skull. I screamed and beat at it with my fists, but the thing was senseless and unstoppable. Something took hold of my ankles and pulled. I was dragged away from the larva and its mouth, dragged right out of the cell. I scrambled to my feet. I turned.

Facing me was the shape from all my nightmares. It was the thing I'd never looked at, standing waiting at the foot of my bed. But now it was right in front of me and I couldn't look away. My throat felt welded together. I couldn't breathe or make a sound.

It had no face, not really. Just a hint of one, like a little kid's scribbles inside a circle. The rest of it didn't even seem to have arms or legs, although in some shadowy fold of its body, I saw the flash of my knife.

The dark figure strode toward me, and I tensed, waiting for that sharpest of blades to go through me. I flinched as the knife lifted, but it stopped and seemed to hover in thin air. Around the handle I saw the shadowy suggestion of a hand. A hand with only four fingers, strangely splayed like a pincer.

"The knife man," I said.

"Mr. Nobody," he replied. "Take it."

Gratefully I took the knife back into my hand.

"We've got to be quick," he said.

He grabbed hold of me and pulled. I had to run to keep up. I realized we were not in the queen's nest outside my house—not the nest with the baby. This one was

huge, like a cathedral of little empty cells, row after row, higher and higher. We were in the massive attic nest.

"Where are they all?" I asked. "The wasps?"

"Getting ready to carry their baby inside. And move yours out."

We were rushing along narrow ridges, leaping over small canyons of cells. I didn't know where we were going.

"But . . . where am I . . . my body really?"

"In the bathtub, unconscious and dying."

"But I'm not dead yet." It was as much a demand as a question.

"You're still alive."

We ran on through the maze of the nest. He seemed to know where he was going.

"But how are you here?" I called after him. "Are you . . ."

"Alive? No. I move in people's dreams mostly. I have to choose who can see me. Hurry now."

I thought of him on my front lawn, the knife guy with his big scary blade, but our neighbor hadn't even seen him. None of them had. Only us. An unsettling thought suddenly came to me.

"That wasn't you, all these years, at the end of my bed?" I asked.

"No. That was only your imagination."

"Oh. Good."

"I only come to warn people, if I can."

"About the wasps?"

I could see more of a shape to him now as he ran, shoulders, arms, legs.

"Yes."

"But who are you really?" I asked.

"Just Mr. Nobody. I was replaced."

I staggered after him, stunned. "It . . . it happened to you?"

"Many years ago."

A wasp suddenly lunged toward us. My knife flashed out and cut the creature into twitching halves.

"I'm not alive," said Mr. Nobody. "Scarcely was. The wasps can disperse me. I can't fight them. I can only give you the knife. And show you the way."

"You mean the way out?"

We'd reached the outer wall of the vast nest, and I could see a bright narrow tunnel boring through the rafters of our house.

I suddenly realized where we were. "This goes into the other nest, doesn't it?"

"Yes."

"What do we need to do?"

"The nest can't function without its queen."

"And what about Theo?"

"To save him you will have to kill the queen."

"Me?"

"It has to be you. I'm nothing."

He was crawling on all fours into the tunnel. I followed. We arrived at a small ledge, the spot I'd become so familiar with after all my visits. Light shafted up from the narrow hole at the bottom of the nest. Hanging from its stalk was the upside-down baby, blinking and wailing. At the top of the nest a small team of wasps was frantically chewing away at the stalk. Taut from the baby's weight, it slowly started to fray.

And beneath the baby was a vast swarm of wasps, as dense as a thundercloud, landing all over it, their wings churning to take its weight.

Suddenly the queen was hovering before us, her stinger cocked high. Her long antennae snaked out and grazed me and Mr. Nobody.

"Oh, not you again," she said dismissively to Mr. Nobody. "Honestly, some people do hold a grudge. Ladies! Over here, please!"

Wasps boiled up through the nest and instantly coated Mr. Nobody.

"Stop it!" I yelled. "Stop!"

With my knife I slashed at them. Bodies fell everywhere, but there were too many, a thousand spots of pale light—and I remembered that dream, the very first night I'd seen the wasps and thought they were angels. There had been a dark shape in the beginning of that dream, and I'd assumed it was my nightmare, but really it'd been only Mr. Nobody come to warn me, and the wasps had obliterated him, just like they were doing now, until his shadow was gone entirely. The writhing mass of wasps dispersed suddenly, as if instructed.

Only the queen remained, hovering before me, a

long antenna just touching the top of my head, the rest of her well beyond my reach. I swiped at her antenna, and each time she deftly lifted it higher, returning it only to speak to me.

"Oh, do put down the knife," she said. "Stop being silly! Look. We're just going to carry the baby in now."

It was impossible not to look. The hole at the bottom of the nest was dilating, letting more wasps fly inside to clamber over the baby's head and shoulders and arms. They would carry him right down out of the nest, through the open window, and into the empty crib.

"There's nothing you can do," the queen said. "You're dying, Steven. In a few seconds you'll be just another Mr. Nobody!"

"I'm not dead yet," I whispered.

She cocked her head. "You're right; you're not."

And in a single swift movement, she swiveled in

midair and plunged her stinger into me. It went right through my chest, right through my heart and out between my shoulder blades.

"There you go," she said. "That should do it."

I felt the venom seeping in, and everything else out: my air, my thoughts, my strength. I was aware of a distant thumping, getting slower and slower.

My body started to jerk, and I dimly realized that the queen was trying to twitch me off her stinger.

"Get off!" she said peevishly. "Stop being difficult!"

I wasn't doing it on purpose. My legs had buckled and I'd fallen to my knees, dragging the queen closer to me.

"Come along now! Off you get!"

Fainter and more irregular, my faraway heart seemed to thump out a final message: *Go ahead . . . and die . . . go . . . a-head . . . aaaaand—*

I thought, *Theo.*

I thought, *Get a grip.*

With what seemed like incredible slowness, I lifted the knife high and plunged it into the queen's back. I held on tight as she shrieked and flew up into the air, taking me with her, still impaled on her stinger.

She tilted and thrashed, trying to throw me off. Her wings battered my head. I held on, one hand on the knife, the other clutching a long hind leg. We flew past the baby's arm. I did not know where my strength came from. With a great wrench I dragged myself higher up onto her back, feeling her stinger snap clean off her abdomen, still lodged inside me.

One of her long antennae came poking back, prodding, trying to find me, trying to find out what exactly was happening to her body.

"Get off!" she screamed.

I grabbed hold of her antenna, yanked it toward

me, and wrapped it round and round my wrist. I felt her fury and terror, like an electric current, through that antenna. It all came coursing out of her in a stream of the foulest language I'd ever heard. It was like beholding her for the first time.

I pulled the knife from her body, plunged it in again fast, higher up, and dragged myself toward her head.

"Don't hurt my baby!" she begged.

"I'd never do anything to hurt my baby!" I yelled, and I sank the knife into her neck and sawed and sawed until her head came away and fell. Tangled in her antenna, I fell with it.

I heard one last great heart thump in my head, and then nothing as I plunged down through the nest. I saw the worker wasps swirling chaotically. Leaderless, they whirled away from the cracking stalk, swirling away from the baby they were sup-posed to be carrying.

The baby started to fall, and I fell alongside its perfect face, down toward the dilating hole in the nest and into the light.

WITH A GASP I OPENED MY EYES, AND THERE were Mr. Nobodys all around me, powerful looming shadows. One of them had huge flat hands held high above me and was chanting like a holy man raising someone from the dead.

"Steven!" I heard someone shout, and then again, "Steve! Steve!"

I felt my heart surge, and it almost swallowed me with blackness again. I blinked and gasped and looked around in terror at all the shadows. They were beginning to have faces now, and bright yellow-and-orange suits, and the one closest to me was taking off his huge flat hands, which were metal paddles.

I was shirtless, shivering.

"He's in rhythm," someone said.

"Let's get him to the ER," another voice said.

"Oh, Steven!" came a more familiar voice.

"Get that stretcher over here!"

"There's wasps in the house!" I croaked.

"Take hold of the drip. Let's move him."

"It's all right," someone said to me. "We've taken care of that."

"The baby," I said. "Theo."

"Baby's fine. You saved his life. The baby's just fine."

And then I must've slept again, because when I woke up, I was someplace different, and I felt calmer, and there were only Mom and Dad beside me. Mom was holding the baby.

I came home the next day. There were still a couple of news vans outside, and reporters tried to talk to us as we walked to the front door, but Dad told them no.

I knew what had happened. They'd told me at the hospital.

The emergency operator I'd called had actually sent a cruiser around to our house, and the two officers had knocked on the door but hadn't seen anything weird. They'd been about to leave, when the dispatcher had gotten another call, an anonymous one this time, saying there were wasps swarming around the house.

"Was it the knife guy who called them?" I'd asked.

"Why would it be the knife guy?" Dad had said.

"I just thought . . . I heard his bell when I was inside the bathroom."

The police had taken another look around back,

and this time they'd seen a huge swarm outside the upstairs bathroom window. They'd called the fire department right away; they'd never seen anything like it.

The firefighters arrived and were getting their helmets on just as Mom arrived back home. She told them the baby and I were inside, and she let them in. They found me unconscious in the bathtub, hunched over the baby, wasps all around me. But almost instantly the wasps flew away, out the broken window.

The baby had been stung only twice. It was amazing, they said. That with all those thousands of wasps, the baby was stung only twice.

I was in real trouble, though. I was all swollen, and my throat was starting to close up, and the paramedics jabbed me full of adrenaline and antihistamines, but my heart stopped anyway.

They got out their de-fib paddles and jolted me back to life.

I was dead for twenty-five seconds.

On Saturday morning Theo had his heart operation. I was still pretty swollen up and freaky-looking, but I wanted to go with Dad and Nicole that evening to see him. There were lots of tubes in him. He looked so small. But the doctors said it had gone really well, and he was strong.

"He'll make a full recovery," the surgeon told us all. "He'll be here only a couple more days."

"And after that we go home and everything goes back to normal," Nicole said cheerfully.

I saw Dad look at Mom, and I wondered what he was thinking. Maybe he was thinking, *The heart is just one problem, but there are lots of others.* Maybe he was thinking, *Things will never be normal.* Maybe, like me, he was thinking we'd never know what was going to happen next week or month or year, but no one really did anyway.

Dad said, "Yeah, it'll be good to get home, won't it?"

"And there's no such thing as normal anyway," I said.

Surprised, Dad's eyes met mine. He gave a tired smile and nodded.

The exterminator came by again a couple of days after Theo's operation, just to make sure there were no other signs of infestation.

Last Friday, his team had spent a solid day shoveling the evacuated nest out of our attic. It had filled fifty garbage bags. They'd also sprayed down the timbers with some kind of chemical to make sure no other wasps would try to build there.

"Odd-looking things," the exterminator said

during his second visit, when he came down from his final check in the crawl space. In his cupped hand he held a few dead pale wasps.

"Have you ever seen that kind before?" I asked.

He was an older man, said he'd been in the business his whole life. He frowned like he'd tasted something nasty, and gave a grunt. "Maybe just once. A long time ago."

I followed him outside as he checked the exterior. The nest above Theo's room had been blasted off the wall with a fire hose. It still lay in crumpled pieces on the ground.

"Now, this is very strange," he said. "See this? You look inside—no cells. The queen didn't lay any eggs in this one. It's just an empty shell. Nothing."

After he left, I picked through the pieces of the nest. I stared hard. There was no sign that a baby had ever grown against those sodden walls. I was about to let the last shard drop, when something caught my eye. A little glint. I looked more closely. Caught in the fibrous weave was a tiny pale rectangle with rounded edges—the smallest, most perfect fingernail I'd ever seen. When I pulled it out, it felt just like wet paper, ready to tear. I dug a little hole in the ground and buried it.

That night in bed I was more tired than I'd ever been.

I tried to do my two lists, but I knew I'd never make it through both.

So I said: "I'm grateful for all the things on this first list."

And I said: "I want everyone on this second list to be okay. And Mr. Nobody, too. And especially Theo."

Before sleep took me, I thought I heard the sound of Mr. Nobody's handbell, and I knew we'd never see him again. I heard Theo murmuring, and Mom talking to him gently as she fed him a bottle.

I pulled the covers over my head and went to sleep in my nest.